THE CHRISTMAS PARTY

Also by Christopher Alston
The Road

THE CHRISTMAS PARTY

Christopher Alston

Aurora Books
Sussex, England

Aurora Books
is an imprint of
The Book Guild Ltd.

The Book Guild Limited
25 High Street
Lewes, Sussex

First published 1994
© Christopher Alston 1994

Set in Baskerville

Typesetting by Dataset
St Leonards-on-Sea, Sussex

Printed in Great Britain by
Antony Rowe Ltd
Chippenham, Wiltshire

A catalogue record for this book is
available from the British Library

ISBN 0 86332 913 6

To Gemma, my devoted and faithful companion, who rarely leaves my side.

PROLOGUE

I dislike being away for Christmas as a rule, but this year, 1956, Julia had promised Diney that we would spend it with her family, who lived in the country a few miles out of Canterbury.

I had of course voiced my dislike of the idea, but Diney was an old school girl-friend of my wife, and we were both god-parents to the children. So I eventually allowed myself to be persuaded.

Unusually for that time of year, although according to legendary ideas and Christmas cards, very correct, it had been snowing hard for the last two days, and we had almost decided to go by train. But Christmas Eve turned out to be a glorious sunny day with a crisp nip in the air, and so, after ensuring that the roads were clear, we set off by car.

Both of us were strangers to that part of Kent, but we were all right as long as we stuck to the great winding arterial roads. Diney had told us to turn off to the right about seven miles from Canterbury and head for a place called Brush.

All was plain sailing and the day was delightful. However, at Tilbury we were delayed at the ferry, and on reaching the Kent side, Julia said that she needed a cup of tea, and as I too felt a bit jaded after waiting about at the ferry, we stopped at a small cafe.

'We mustn't be too long as we don't want to miss the road and it will be dark before we reach Diney's anyway,' Julia remarked.

'All right, dear, half an hour and then we'll be off again.'

It was, however, four o'clock before we cleared Gravesend, and we pushed ahead as fast as we could, although we were using our headlights a little while later, and it was six o'clock before we neared the old city of Canterbury.

'We should be turning off the main road soon, you'd better keep your eyes peeled for the signposts from now on.'

'Yes.' My wife glanced up from Diney's letter that she had taken from her bag and was reading with the aid of a torch. 'She says here that it's a secondary road, in fact not much more than a lane, but that there's a church on the opposite side of the main road just before the turning.'

'Well that's a help at any rate, but I wish we hadn't left it so late.' I continued to stare into the distance ahead. The air was frosty and the snow on the verges sparkled in the light of the headlights. The roofs of houses were thickly coated in white, and warm friendly gleams of light beckoned from behind curtained windows. Silhouetted behind many were Christmas decorations, and I began to wish that we were snugly behind our own curtains. However, I thought, it's bound to be cheerful at Diney's.

My thoughts were interrupted by Julia who had spotted what seemed to be an old church tower caught for a moment in the headlights, and as I slowed down we came abreast of its lychgate.

'That must be it,' she exclaimed, and as we drove slowly past. 'Yes! Darling, there's the signpost.'

8

I saw the signpost at the same time as she and swung the car off the main road into what was barely more than a lane carpeted in snow.

'Doesn't look as if a snowplough has ever been up here, nor for that matter any other traffic.' I spoke anxiously, as the only tracks in the snow appeared to be those of bicycles and pedestrians.

However, the snow was crisp and the car crunched steadily along between snow-laden branches which overhung the lane, making it appear almost like a tunnel. We eventually cleared this and came out into the open country, with great open fields completely carpeted in white as far as the eye could see. The road skirted the edge of a hill and in the valley below a light winked from an isolated cottage.

'Seems to be miles from anywhere,' Julia remarked a trifle anxiously, 'but it must have been the right turning. Oh Lord, here's a fork in the road; now which way do we go?'

'Does Diney give any more directions in her letter?' I had slowed down as we approached the road junction. 'The trouble with this snow is that you can't tell which is the main road and which is the by-road.'

I got out, stamping my feet to get them warm. It was a beautiful, clear, cold night, the moon's light accentuating the whiteness of the fields, bathing the whole countryside in its pale rays.

I walked up to the road junction to try and find which fork to take. Both lanes seemed similar in size and both little used.

Just as I turned back to the car, I heard the whistle of a train in the distance. It seemed to me to be a cheery sort of whistle, but perhaps this was because I was glad to know that something else was travelling across the apparently deserted countryside, as well as us.

'Can you see the train Julia?' I asked as I returned to the car. My wife got out and was pointing away to the left in the direction we had come.

'Over there, you can see the glare from the smoke-stack.'

I saw it then too. And behind the engine the gleam of light from the carriages. It seemed to be emerging from a tunnel.

I made up my mind. 'We'll take the left fork, darling. Perhaps there's a station somewhere down in the valley.'

'Yes, I think perhaps you're right. It doesn't seem a very important line, and it is a very short train from what I can see of it.'

I glanced back to see that it was almost directly below us, and, as Julia had said, seemed to be quite a short train; two or three carriages long at most.

As we set off again it disappeared round the shoulder of the hill and we followed as best we could. I glanced at Julia. 'If there is a station we can ask the way. Somebody will be bound to know the Old Grange.'

As we rounded the next bend we heard the engine's whistle again and saw it was slowing down; a little further on we could now make out some more lights.

'It looks as if there's a station or halt of some kind up there,' I said.

Julia shivered. 'I do hope so. Do you realize that we haven't seen a soul since we left the main road. It seems quite another world up here. And it's getting jolly cold, too.'

The road took a sharp bend and we passed over the railway line, and there beneath us the train was drawing into a small railway station dimly lit by old-fashioned candle lanterns. From a quick glance it looked to be deserted and little used.

The road took another sharp bend to the left and downwards, and we found ourselves in a tiny station yard, surrounded by high hedges. On our left was the back of what appeared to be the wooden ticket office and waiting room.

'Look, darling, over there.' Julia had grasped my arm and pointed to the other side of the yard. I had already slowed right down and now stopped the car just short of the single platform which formed a continuation of the yard.

Then I saw and heard it too. The stamping of horses' hooves and the muffled jingle of harness, and there, lined up one behind the other, were three old-fashioned coaches, each drawn by a pair of horses. I could see the dull gleam of their brass carriage lamps, and the muffled figures of their grooms standing by the horses' heads to quieten the animals as the little engine came to a wheezing halt at the platform.

This was something so out of the ordinary that I could do nothing but stare. To see one coach might possibly stir one's curiosity, but to see three all at once was a novelty, and extremely impressive.

My attention was drawn back to the train by Julia's tug at my arm. I had barely time to notice the funny little engine with a high smoke stack and the barely visible letters 'E.V.' half obliterated on the cab, when the doors were being opened and a babble of voices filled the little station yard with cheerful chatter and happy laughter.

Both carriages were spilling their occupants upon the platform and the porter was alternately bowing to the travellers and helping them with their baggage.

'Darling, who are they? Is it a touring company of actors? Why are they dressed like that?'

Julia might well ask, for all these people were dressed in old-fashioned clothes. all of them were young. The ladies wore long skirted travelling cloaks and bonnets, and the men high collared coats and tall hats, some with buttoned gaiters and others with buckled shoes. All seemed in a festive mood.

'There must be a fancy-dress ball somewhere in the vicinity,' I answered. 'Anyway, when the porter has seen the carriages off we'll ask the way.'

As I was speaking, the travellers had boarded the three vehicles, the doors were closed and the coach-men now cracked their whips with a flourish. The first coach rumbled out of the yard and on down the hill, followed by the other two. We could hear the muffled clatter of the hooves, and the jingle of the harnesses as they disappeared into the night.

The station seemed lonely and deserted when they had left and this was even more noticeable as the little engine began to wheeze, and with clouds of steam drew noisily away from the platform. The place was now as still and quiet as the proverbial graveyard. We approached the solitary figure of the porter who seemed to be gazing rather disconsolately in the direction the carriages had taken.

I approached him. 'Excuse me.' He turned vaguely towards me as if only just sensing my presence. I was rather startled by the pallor of his face, probably accentuated by the reflection of the moon. He, too, seemed to be dressed in an odd sort of way, wearing a heavy coat with a high collar. I remember thinking that this must be a very out-of-the-way railway line not yet nationalized into British Railways.

'Excuse me,' I began again, 'perhaps you could tell

12

me if we are on the right road for the Old Grange –
Commander Harrison's house. We were told to take
the Brush road, but we're not quite sure if we are on
the right one.'

The porter glanced at me with a sort of vague,
troubled look in his eye. Then he stretched out his
arm and pointed in the direction the carriages had
taken. And then, without a word, he turned about
and made his way back to the ticket office.

I stared blankly after him for a moment. The fellow
hadn't been rude. It seemed rather that his thoughts
were not with us. Rather that he was still with his
cheerful travellers and that we didn't exist except to
his senses. It was a weird feeling and difficult to
describe. Julia and I might have been alone on the
platform and imagined it all, except that the wheel-
marks of the carriages were still there and a pile of
dung where one of the horses had stood steamed in
the chilly air.

Julia had wandered off and now called me. She was
pointing to the signboard on the platform. She had
wiped away the snow and as I joined her I could just
make out the name in faded letters: 'Brush Halt', and
underneath, 'Elam Valley Line'.

My wife suddenly shivered. 'Darling, let's get on
our way.' She took my arm and we walked back to the
car. 'There's something spooky about all this,' she
continued as we got in, 'and it's terribly lonely here'.

I tried to reassure her. 'Oh, I don't know, it's all
right. But it's very odd about those travellers.' And
although I did not say any more, I too was quite glad
to get on our way now that the yard was deserted and
the cheery chatter of the travellers had gone.

We took the same direction as the carriages and this
time found no further road junctions to confuse the

drive, and in no more than fifteen minutes we found what we were looking for. The Old Grange was a lovely late Georgian mansion, and as we came to the brick wall enclosing its small park, Julia recognized it from the description Diney had given her.

Five minutes later we were warming ourselves by a huge old-fashioned log fire and I was enjoying a large whisky and soda that the commander had brought me; he was a big, cheerful fellow, with an infectious laugh, although from experience I knew he could be as serious-minded as anyone.

Diney was looking lovely, and as usual I found myself admiring her wonderful eyes. She and Julia were chatting away together over their sherry as only two females will when they have not seen each other for a year.

'You managed to find your way here, then,' the commander was saying. 'I am afraid we live a bit off the beaten track, but it's well worth it if you like old houses, and this one is steeped in tradition.'

I told him that we had been a bit foxed when we came to the fork in the road. 'The trouble is,' I continued, 'the roads look so alike under this snow, and it's difficult to tell which is the right one. In the end we asked the way at the station.'

'Oh,' he said, 'and what station was that?'

'A funny little out-of-the-way place a few miles down the road. It didn't seem to do much business but curiously enough a trainload of people dressed up for a fancy dress ball steamed in as we drove up. As a matter of fact it was by following the train to the station that we came on the right road.'

The commander was silent for a moment, his forehead creased in a somewhat bewildered frown. Then he called across to Diney.

14

'Darling, do you know of a station a few miles down the road? I didn't even know there was a railway running near here.'

'Julia was just telling me about it, and the three horse-drawn carriages full of people dressed in funny clothes. I must say I didn't know there was a large house party going on locally.'

The commander and I went over to the two girls who were sitting on stools by the fireplace. I described the carriages to my host who scratched his head, perplexed.

'Of course,' Diney continued, 'there was a small loop line here some years ago – oh, well before the war, called the something or other Valley Line. I believe its terminus was at Dover and it wandered around this district and finally arrived at Faversham. But I am none too sure of my facts. There was an old station at Brush, I believe, but the tracks were pulled up some time ago, so you couldn't have seen a train there.'

'Well, there was definitely a train, no doubt at all about that,' Julia assured them, 'and Ian and I saw the people getting out.'

'We'll take your word for it anyway,' laughed the commander. 'Tell you what, let's have a drive round after morning service tomorrow and see if you can show us this railway of yours. It will be something to do and give us an appetite for lunch.'

Just then dinner was served and there was plenty to talk about, especially between the two women who chattered about their school days.

We went to bed early that night and slept soundly, although I must confess that I dreamed about the funny little train and its occupants. And once during the middle of the night I think I woke, and to this

15

day I swear I heard again the muffled clatter of the hooves and the jingle of harness, though at the time I sleepily thought that the fancy dress ball was over and the guests were returning home.

Next morning after the Christmas Day Service in the village church, we set off to look for our railway station, which we found no trouble in locating. As we swung into the yard it all seemed quite familiar, but somehow different.

The ticket office and waiting room were now converted into a small cottage, and the yard and platform were covered with weeds, partially hidden by the snow. The snow was clearly disturbed by wheeltracks, and the little pile of dung was still where the horses had stood. Yet when we went onto the platform, we saw that there was no railway line, just a virgin whiteness of snow between the embankments which disappeared into a tunnel of snow-covered trees.

1

Julian Farley stood at the tall windows of his study proudly taking in the newly-created terrace and the avenue planted with young beech trees. To his left workmen were putting the final touches to the recently constructed east wing, and to his right was the magnificent conservatory in which he hoped to indulge his hobby of collecting tropical plants.

Although Brush Hall belonged to his wife, Viscountess Alice having inherited it from her own father, he thought of it as his own and was determined to leave his mark on it.

His wife was the widow of the late Colonel Viscount Emmerdale who had died after the battle of Waterloo, and he had courted her ardently, determined to improve himself and become part of the aristocracy of his country.

He was the son of a north country industrialist who owned a foundry and iron works. He was ambitious and inventive, and the birth of the railway mania gave him the opportunity to realize his ambition. The early days of railway building saw the locomotives running on rails of wrought iron, but as their weight and speed increased these rails soon began to wear far too quickly. He sought out the great rail engineer, Robert Stephenson, with the suggestion that the latest type of hardened steel should be tried. Steel was something of an experimental material and being a great deal more expensive than iron had found few adherents so far. Stephenson was very impressed with the young man's ideas and agreed that a limited length of railway should be tried.

Julian had gambled on the successful outcome of the experiment and persuaded his father to switch to steel production, producing steel rails, so that in a short while, when Robert Stephenson was convinced that steel was by far the superior material, the Farley Works were ready to supply the new rails. And what Robert Stephenson did others engineers were wont to follow.

And so it was not long before Julian Farley became a very rich man, and still being ambitious decided to join other entrepreneurs in the mania that was sweeping Britain as new rail lines were being laid all over the country. A partial slump eventually followed when the government became more particular and enforced a far stricter system for granting bills authorizing the building of speculative rail tracks.

As a result Julian decided to move to the south of the country where new opportunities seemed more lucrative, with communications yet to be built between London and the south and west coast ports. So far a large concern, the South Eastern Railway seemed to hold the monopoly, and so Julian Farley looked for a route with which he could challenge this monopoly.

He also realized that although extremely wealthy, his north country roots and his somewhat humble origins were a disadvantage when it came to attracting financial and political backing. And so he cast around for means to improve his social background.

He was still unmarried mainly because he had never had the inclination to settle down, his life to date having been dedicated to pursuing new business and making money.

Thinking along these lines he decided that now was perhaps the time to find a suitable wife whose station in life could improve his social status, and give him an entry to houses and families where he had hitherto been thwarted.

Little did he realize that these thoughts were to bear fruit far sooner than he had anticipated. For one day when he paid a visit to the construction camp where his new railway line was forging ahead in Kent, the incident that was to change his whole life occurred. He had obtained by Act of Parliament a bill to construct a line from Strood to Faversham and then onwards to Dover, hoping to wrest the continental mail contract from his much larger rivals, the South Eastern Railway. He was later to take the line into London.

The line had reached the outskirts of the small Kentish village of Brush where a slight rise in the terrain gave a good view of the countryside and as usual there was considerable activity going on. A small engine was being used to shunt materials to the head of the line with much puffing accompanied by shrieks from its strident whistle.

Suddenly there were shouts from several of the gang, and breaking off his conversation with the gang foreman Julian looked up to see the cause of the furore. He noticed that several of the men were pointing across the neighbouring field where a lane ran parallel to the course of the line. He immediately picked out the drama which attracted the workmen. Careering down the lane was a small pony trap, quite

19

out of control; the pony had obviously been frightened by the engine's whistle. A slight figure of a woman
could be seen pulling on the reins desperately trying
to slow the animal's panic-stricken progress. Even as
he watched the trap reached a slight bend in the lane
and such was its speed that it slewed sideways and
with a splintering crash, quite audible to the watchers,
struck a roadside oak tree and turned on its side thus
effectively halting the run-away pony.

Shouting to the men to follow, Julian vaulted onto
his horse. Charging down the incline and across the
field he cleared the hedge at its far side and reached
the scene of the accident in no time at all. Jumping
from the saddle he reached the side of the still figure
of the woman who had been thrown from the trap
when it overturned.

Gently he turned her so that her head was clear of
the mud, and supported her in his arms. She was of
slight build and dressed in smart country clothes. He
was relieved to see she was breathing shallowly
although she was very pale. By now a bunch of
workmen arrived on the scene and one of them
exclaimed, 'That's the Lady Emmerdale from the big
house,' at which Julian looked askance, never having
heard of her.

Just as he was wondering what to do next, her
eyelids flickered open and he found himself looking
at the palest of grey eyes not twelve inches from his,
and heard her whisper, 'What has happened, what
am I doing here?' And then, 'My poor Dobbin, is he
all right?' Presuming that she was referring to the
pony he glanced round to see that he was standing
quietly by the broken-shafted trap, although still
shivering from shock.

'Quite all right, my lady, but I fear your trap is

20

badly damaged. But how do you feel? Here take a sip of this.' Producing his hip flask he held it to her mouth, lifting her head to assist her in drinking. After a few swallows he could see some colour returning to her cheeks.

'You are very kind sir, I should be obliged if you could help me up; perhaps you could find me something to sit on.'

By now a horse and cart had arrived from the camp, and gathering the slight figure easily into his arms Julian lifted her onto the seat. Meanwhile the carter, well versed with horses, was examining Dobbin, and having cut away the traces, led him over.

'Nothing amiss with him, ma'am, only frightened I dare say. Not used to locomotive whistles I expect.'

'Poor darling,' she held out her hand to which the animal responded, nuzzling the fingers.

'We must get you home, your ladyship. I am afraid it will have to be on this cart as we have nothing better available, but I dare say we can make you fairly comfortable.' So saying, Julian climbed up beside her supporting her as best he could whilst the carter joined them on the other side and gathered up the reins. 'Now if you can point us in the right direction, ma'am, we'll take it nice and easy and you'll soon be comfortable in your own home.'

Julian gave instructions to the men to fetch a wagon and load up the broken trap and follow in due course, and then with Dobbin trailing behind on a lead they set off to Brush Hall which Julian learned was her home.

Following the lane as instructed they soon came to the imposing iron gates which opened on to a winding drive bordered by trees and shrubs. Julian could not help but notice the untidiness and some-

21

what neglected appearance as they progressed towards the house. Little was said but he could see that the woman was recovering rapidly from her ordeal and he marvelled that such a slight body could prove so resilient.

The drive opened out onto a forecourt of a lovely Queen Anne style mansion, although here again Julian noticed the somewhat unkempt appearance of both house and lawns.

As they approached the house a servant appeared and immediately taking in the scene hurried inside and reappeared with a female seemingly distraught to see her mistress in such circumstances. Both Julian and the carter jumped down, the latter to hold the horse's head while Julian, with a muttered 'please excuse the liberty', lifted the lady off the seat. Holding her in his arms, he called to the servants, 'Your mistress has had an accident! You had best find her somewhere comfortable to lie down and send someone for the doctor.' Without further ado he carried her indoors, following the servants who led him up an imposing staircase to a bedchamber on the first floor, and laid her gently upon the large four-poster bed after the female servant had hastily removed the brocade coverlet and then tucked pillows under the patient's head and shoulders.

Gazing down at her Julian could but marvel at her beauty. She seemed tall and slender although far from thin where it mattered, and her face was beautiful with a fine bone structure. She might well have been in her middle thirties had not the fine wrinkles at her neck and the 'crows feet' at her eyes betrayed her. He was later to learn that she was a few years older than himself.

'I must apologize for my roughness, my lady, and

for not having the opportunity to introduce myself. I am Julian Farley and as you can probably guess from my accent I come from the North Country originally. But here I am in Kent building a railway line hopefully to reach the coast at Dover. I am afraid that it was my locomotive that frightened your pony and I must feel responsible for the accident.'

She beckoned to her servants to help her sit up, smiling up at this large rather rough-cut stranger whose strong arms had brought her here.

'I must thank you for your help and kindness sir. It must be many years since I was carried to my bed-chamber by a gentleman and never before being introduced!' Her smile had something of a roguish sparkle. She went on, 'I am Lady Emmerdale, actually the Dowager Viscountess Emmerdale for what that is worth these days. My late husband, the viscount, never fully recovered from his wounds after Water-loo and died some thirty years ago.' She paused for a moment, her thoughts going back those many years to a time when she was a young woman with a happy life before her, only to have it shattered in the aftermath of war.

'You may call upon me in a day or two when I feel stronger and allow me to thank you in a more fitting manner.' Impulsively Julian picked up one slender hand still muddied from its contact with the soil and brought it to his lips. 'I am yours to command, my lady, and I shall look forward to calling upon you a few days hence and hope to find you quite recovered from your ordeal.'

Leaving the house he found his horse standing in the charge of a groom. The carter had departed and he learned that the pony trap had been delivered. Somewhat bemused he rode slowly back to the camp.

23

He had never met anyone comparable to the viscountess. She was gracious and very beautiful and his thoughts lingered again on the slender body lying on the bed, and he realized that he was very much attracted to her. Of course, she was of noble blood and he a commoner from industrial north. But in spite of that his pulse started to quicken at the thought of seeing her again and he knew he must take advantage of this opportunity. Stranger things had happened, she was a widow and obviously lonely.

As he rode down the drive he found time to look around him. There was no doubt the whole place had a neglected air about it. He realized that a fine house with spacious grounds took a considerable amount of money to upkeep. Either the viscountess had lost interest in her home or more likely the costs of proper maintenance were more than she could afford. He decided that whilst he was in the neighbourhood he would make some discreet inquiries. He did not realize how quickly his thoughts were jumping ahead. But here was the opportunity that he had been thinking about latterly. The viscountess could open the doors to a more complete social life for which he had been craving and after all he was rich, and if all went well with the railway he would be a great deal richer.

True to his thoughts he made enquiries and learned more about the owner of Brush Hall. The viscountess was something of a recluse and had been since her husband died ten years after being horribly wounded at the battle of Waterloo. She had two sons. One was about forty years old, the present viscount, and in a mental institution as a result of a hunting accident when he had fallen from his horse who had then kicked his skull injuring him severely. The younger son was at present fighting in the Crimea. She was seldom seen locally unless out driving in her pony trap and rumour had it that she had difficulty in keeping up the estate as her husband had left her little money, most of which went in paying the institution who looked after her son. She was a little over sixty years old, something which Julian found difficult to believe, and this made her some seven years older than he, not that that mattered as she looked at least ten years younger and was still a very attractive woman.

Two days after the accident Julian called at Brush Hall ostensibly to inquire after the lady's health but in truth because he could wait no longer to see this woman who attracted him so much. It was not only her high class breeding and social standing but also a desire to dominate and claim this noble woman who was so much superior to his own class. He felt a stirring in his loins at the thought of possessing a female such as she, with her slender beauty and quiet grace; to stir her own pulses with his masculinity and to make her desire him and arouse her own sexuality.

He was shown into her boudoir that afternoon, a very feminine room in which he felt grossly out of place and clumsy in his serge suit, stiff collar and cravat. As she rose to greet him he was again struck by her slender form and the incredible smoothness of her skin. The fantastic grey eyes showed a hint of demureness as if she was unused to entertaining a man she hardly knew in her home.

He gave a slight bow and kissed the back of her outstretched hand rather than shake it.

'I am delighted to meet you again, my lady, I trust you are quite recovered from the accident. No bruises I hope?' He went on, 'My engine driver was fearfully upset. He blames himself for being the cause of your pony bolting. Said that he should have known better.'

'Please tell him I absolve him entirely. These things happen I suppose, and I did not realize, myself, that your locomotive possessed such a strident noise, and then again I had forgotten how near your railway line was to the estate. But the railway has arrived and people like me will have to get used to it, not that I agree with these new-fangled machines!' She shrugged her elegant shoulders. 'From what I hear, I have no doubt travel will become much easier.'

Julian was aware that the mania of railway building which had swept the country was not popular with many people especially some of the landed gentry who begrudged the opening up of the countryside.

'I suppose the railways are something of an intrusion but they will benefit everyone eventually. For instance, if my railway reaches Dover on schedule I have every chance of contracting for the continental mail which will certainly improve the postal services to and from Europe.' He continued to extol the benefits which would accrue with the coming of the railway. 'But I forget my manners, my lady, I must not bore you talking business!'

She had been listening without interrupting. She was somewhat intrigued by this large rather rugged man with traces of a north country accent. He was dressed well although the material of his clothes could hardly be called elegant. But his manners were good and she guessed that he was unused to meeting and conversing with the 'upper classes'.

'Let us have some tea and you must tell me how you came to build these railways. If you would be good enough to pull that bell cord Sarah will look after us.' Over cups of tea she encouraged him to tell her about himself and about the railway and he warmed to his subject and became so engrossed that the time passed quickly. At length she rose. 'You must excuse me now Mr. Farley, I am a little tired. But I have not enjoyed a conversation so much for such a long time. You must come again soon, you have done me good and it has been so interesting. I had no idea how life outside these walls was progressing in such exciting ways.'

In the days that followed Julian went over in his mind again and again their conversation and the interest that the viscountess had seemed to take in all that he said. Although she was older then he, she might well have been a younger woman with her somewhat ethereal beauty and her lively conversation, and he was greatly attracted to her as a person and also to her femininity. He dared not dwell too much on any future there might be between them, but he had some considerable wealth which must be something of an asset and he guessed that she was a lonely woman but very 'proper' in her attitudes and a marriage could be advantageous to both.

He could not afford to be coy or shy in his future actions and so, taking advantage of the viscountess's vague invitation, he took to dropping in at Brush Hall on whatever pretext he could invent, and although she probably saw through his excuses she made no attempt to discourage him, in fact quite the opposite, and so it was not many visits later that she started to call him Julian and asked him to use her first name, Alice.

☆ ☆ ☆

Autumn was upon them and the trees were beginning to take on coppery tints as the days became shorter. Julian had been living in Faversham as a temporary headquarters, but as the line progressed beyond Brush following the direction of the Dover road he found himself at too great a distance from the railhead and so he started to look for an inn where he could sleep. He happened to mention this when he had occasion to leave the Hall earlier than was his wont. They were strolling in the rather unkempt garden when she suddenly stopped, putting her hand upon his arm.

'My dear man, I would not hear of it. There is so much room here you can stay at the Hall and make it your headquarters.' She saw his hesitation and gripped his arm tighter. 'If you are thinking of the proprieties you need not. I think that I am old enough not to let that concern me, besides which the servants can be chaperones!'

He put his hand over hers and squeezed her fingers gently and she made no attempt to withdraw them. 'My lady, Alice, I mean, I should like that very much. It would be really delightful to see you every evening, and to tell the truth I get awfully bored in my present lodgings with no one to talk to.' He was about to add something about his cold bed, but thought better of it. Best not rush things he thought, he must be patient, although looking at her delightfully attractive features he knew that this would not be easy. Maybe something in his look communicated itself to her as a slight flush rose to her cheeks and she slowly withdrew her hand from his and continued to walk along the terrace. Without looking at him she went on to say that she would make arrangements to have a room ready and that she would look forward to seeing him in time for dinner.

Fate was being good to him. He was certain now that he would be able to persuade the viscountess to marry him and he, in his turn, would use his money to renovate the house and gardens to their former elegance. All the following day his mind was in a ferment with plans for the future and time would not pass quickly enough in his anticipation of making his home at Brush Hall.

He liked to spend much of his time at the railhead. It was unusual for the owner of a line to be chief engineer as well but he was well qualified, having learned the trade under Robert Stephenson the architect of the foremost railways in the north of England. But he liked to accompany the surveyors planning the actual route, which of course involved him with the landowners over whose property his line would run. He also spent time at Dover arranging the construction of the terminus at the end of the line. Although it was by no means a one man company he knew that to lead from the front meant a successful venture.

He arranged for his baggage to be sent on ahead to Brush Hall and when he arrived in good time for dinner his room had been made ready and his clothes unpacked. The viscountess herself showed him his room and the geography of the house, pointing out the amenities and indicating, a trifle shyly, where her bed-chamber was, situated at some distance from his.

The meal was not formal and the maid Sarah brought in the dishes and then left the room, so that they were free to talk, although it was Julian who held forth about his work and his hopes for the future. It was plain that she was impressed both with his aspirations and with the man himself. She had never come into contact with someone in that walk of life, his rugged good looks intrigued her and his masculinity stirred an emotion which at her age she had not expected to feel again. For it was many years since her husband had died and living the life of a semi-recluse as she did had not sought or looked for any involvement. With one son, Gerald, in an institution, and the other, Jeremy, a cavalry officer fighting in the Crimea, she had become used to a solitary and uneventful life, until Julian had arrived on the scene.

After drinking their coffee and chatting awhile, she excused herself, saying that she liked to retire early as she enjoyed the birds with their dawn chorus, especially at this time of year. 'But you sit as long as you wish, Julian.'

He rose with her, looking down at her upturned face and fighting a growing desire to kiss her lips. 'Good night Alice, sleep well and thank you again for asking me to stay in your house. I shall not stay up long either.' He contented himself with raising her hand and kissing it.

As he sat comfortably finishing a cigar his thoughts turned towards his railway. Until he had met Alice, as he now thought of her, all his waking hours were completely wrapped up with his future plans and the success of his railway reaching Dover. But why stop there? Why not a railway right along the south coast? Until now Brunel, the other great innovator of rail and canal engineering, had assumed a monopoly in the south and west with his broad gauge lines. A competitive line to take in the south coast towns, which Brunel's did not, might well prove a successful venture if he could raise the finance and obtain a Bill authorized by parliament.

Lying in bed he was very aware of the occupant of the bedroom along the corridor. He must pursue his amorous advances and overcome Alice's inherent shyness. He was quite sure that she was attracted to him, but whether she would wish to change her whole mode of life and share her home with him was something he had yet to find out. The line could do without him for a day or two and he would spend more time with her.

The next day he travelled back to Faversham on the work train and called at a livery stable, inquiring where he might purchase a conveyance. After viewing various carriages he bought a cabriolet and a fine grey gelding, and arranged for them to be delivered to the railway station where a flat car and a box would be waiting to transport them to Brush Hall. Then another thought occurred to him. If he was going to live at Brush Hall, something on which he was determined, he would have a station built where the line bypassed the village. Just a small stopping off station with its own yard and facilities. This would surprise Alice and he would not mention it until his future at Brush was finalized. His mind was a whirl with plans and he was restless for the accomplishment of his schemes.

The following day he met the train with the cabriolet and horse aboard and after unloading and harnessing up he drove off to the admiring remarks of his foreman. Although he had said nothing his men were aware of what was afoot and were unanimous in their approval.

Arriving at the Hall he espied Alice in the garden. Hearing the arrival of the carriage she looked up in surprise. Recognizing him, a slow smile spread across her face.

'Where did you get that fine cabriolet, Julian? And what a fine animal! He's lovely'. She fondled the horse's muzzle.

'Come on, Alice, let us go for a drive and you can show me the countryside and teach me to drive properly.' She stood back, better to admire the carriage with its elegantly curved bodywork and folding hood, which was 'half-struck' as a protection against rain and sunglare, and provided some privacy from prying eyes. There was also a rigid leather apron to protect the legs and the shafts were curved, giving the whole carriage a pleasing look. 'I'll just go and fetch a bonnet and scarf. I shall only be a minute.'

They set off down the drive, a little bell on the horse's collar tinkling merrily and giving some warning of their passage. When they had turned into the lane towards the village Alice again complimented him on the choice of horse.

'If you relax on the reins, Julian, he will find his own pace and not be pulling; ah, you see he goes with quite a flourish.'

Indeed they continued at a spanking trot, and as they approached the houses their inhabitants appeared, with the men doffing their hats and the women giving little curtsys, all smiling when they recognized the viscountess. Julian was as proud as punch to have her beside him. He saluted with his whip and raised his own hat whilst Alice waved happily not the least embarrassed to be seen with such a handsome gentleman. Spontaneously he caught her hand and kissed it and she responded by placing her other hand on his. Replacing the whip in its holder he changed hands on the reins and put his left arm about her shoulders, squeezing gently.

'Julian, you will give me a bad name,' she remonstrated happily. He hastily removed his arm apologizing.

'Forgive me, Alice, but I am so happy I got quite carried away. I am not used to being seen in the company of such a lovely lady, this must be the happiest day of my life.'

'It has been a long time since anyone paid me such a charming compliment, my dear, I do not mind at all really, and anyway it's many a long year since I have driven through the village, we must do it often.' He glanced at her and slowly her lovely face coloured in a slow blush and she rested her head on his shoulder. They were now past the houses and Julian slowed and then halted the horse. Putting his arm again around the viscountess he gently drew her unresisting body towards him. He tilted her head up with his fingers and they gazed at each other for a long moment and then he bent towards her and gently kissed her on the lips. At first she failed to respond and he could feel her heart quickening, and then slowly her lips opened, and putting her arms around his neck she held him tight. After a long moment they withdrew, and Julian whispered, 'Marry me Alice, we could be so happy together. I should be so proud to be your husband. There would be nothing that we could not do together. Say you will, dearest.'

She gazed at him fondly. 'My dear, I am so much older than you, in fact I thought that at my age I should never want to love a man again. But I have to admit I have been so happy since I met you and, if you really feel that my age will make no difference nothing would bring me greater joy than sharing the rest of our lives together.'

She was silent for a moment; Julian gathered up the reins clucking the horse into motion. Then she continued in a quietly controlled tone.

'But you will have to be patient with me, my dear, it has to be a marriage of companionship.' She averted her face shyly. 'At my age you must not expect me to find passion in our relationship. You will have to be gentle with me should I be unable to return the ardour that you may expect. I am no shy young thing, but having known no physical contact with a man for so long it will be difficult for me to respond in that way.'

For an answer Julian placed his hand on hers reassuringly. 'To have you by my side will suffice until we know each other's feelings, and your age is no bar to that kind of relationship. When you are ready to make love you will know.' Inwardly he was eager to make that as short a time as possible. To say that he was consumed with lust for this attractive woman would be an exaggeration, but he desired her as a woman and would pursue this end until he had awakened her own bodily demands and would make her wholly his.

Arriving at the house she bade him drive round to the stables. 'We must find a stall for your animal and make him comfortable for the night. Tomorrow he must meet Dobbin and they can graze in the paddock.' Together they unharnessed and Julian pushed the cabriolet into an empty shed, and then found hay and water. 'I will arrange for some fodder to be delivered tomorrow, and Alice, you must allow me to help with these expenses.'

As they entered the house Alice turned to him, her eyes sparkling. 'That was lovely, Julian, such fun to be driven in such a fine turnout and show off in the village. And so romantic to be proposed to in such a way, goodness me I really feel young and so happy, I think I must love you very much, my darling.' They had reached the privacy of her room and Julian reached out and drew her to him unresisting, crushing her slender form and kissing her long and passionately. She was only too well aware of his hardness through the material of her dress and to her wonderment felt excitement rising in her, something she had not been aware she could feel after all these years. She broke away hastily but not before Julian had perceived her reaction to his own passionate physical urge.

'I must go and change.' She meant to cool his obvious ardour. 'This evening we must behave and make our plans in a sensible manner.' And after supper this they did. They would be married in the village church after the banns had been called. 'No point in dilly-dallying, since you are already living here now we might as well conform to propriety and live as man and wife. Although it is most unseemly for someone of my age, I feel I cannot wait for you to make an honest woman of me. Oh darling Julian, that was a wonderful day that you came into my life even if it was caused by a locomotive whistle!' She chuckled happily. 'Just a small wedding, only a few guests; and very quiet and very private, please. Oh dear, who shall I have at my side to give me away?' She chattered on suggesting ideas in an excited way and Julian let her run on, enjoying her happiness.

'How would you like to run up to London on my train?' he asked. 'We could do some shopping. You will need a new outfit which will be my wedding present, and we could go to the theatre if you like, stay the night, see people, whatever you like. Come

35

back next day or stay a bit longer?'

'Oh that would be fun, Julian, and I can see some old friends that I have not met for years. But it would be rather expensive wouldn't it? We cannot stay at the same hotel, that would be most improper! I know, I can stay with Mary, a cousin, I have not seen her for ages. I'll write to her tonight.'

All went according to plan, they shopped together and Julian was introduced to various friends and managed a visit to his broker and bank manager to discuss railway business, and sound them out on the possibility on a promotion for his latest scheme to extend his line. As he told Alice later, he had some very successful meetings.

She thoroughly enjoyed the journey on his special train which he had arranged, so much more comfortable than going by road, she decided. 'It's a wonderful achievement, my dear, I am very proud of you,' she told him.

It was now the end of October, 1854, and the week after they had arrived at Brush Hall, news filtered through that there had been a spectacular battle at Balaclava in the Crimea. With the advent of the discovery of the telegraph machine war news was reaching England far more quickly. Apparently Cardigan had led his cavalry regiments in a glorious charge to capture the Russian guns, but casualties appeared to be heavy.

Worried, the viscountess sought further news.

'My younger son, Jeremy, is a captain in the 17th Lancers, my late husband's regiment. Oh my dear, I hope he is all right. I know that he was attached to Lord Cardigan's division.'

Julian reassured her and said that he would make further inquiries. He discovered that casualties had indeed been high and was later to learn that out of six hundred cavalry officers and other ranks only two hundred had survived the battle and many of those were wounded. Five hundred horses had been lost, and although they captured the guns they could not hold them since in the chaotic muddle by staff officers no infantry were sent to back them up. In fact, rumour was rife that Cardigan had acted against orders.

Alice could see by the gravity of his expression that all was not well and there was no news of her son's fate.

'I've been promised further details as soon as more news is received but I fear that it may not be good,' Julian told her. Alice broke down and placed her head on his chest. After a little she recovered somewhat and murmuring endearments Julisn wiped her eyes. 'Thank God I have you, Julian, I should have been completely distraught had I been alone. I will be brave, maybe Jeremy was only one of the wounded and is in hospital.' Julian did not like to tell her that he doubted whether her son would be any better off as he had learned that the conditions in the hospitals, especially Scutari, the base hospital, were quite appallaing, what with the lack of proper nursing and disease being rampant. The lack of medicines and even bandages did not bear description.

More news filtered through in the days and weeks that followed, and Julian forbore to press his attentions too amorously for fear of upsetting Alice further. Then one day a letter arrived from the War Ministry confirming that Jeremy was alive but severely wounded and in the Scutari base hospital. They also learned that a certain Miss Nightingale and a party of volunteer nurses and further supplies of medicines had arrived in the Crimea, and that she had immediately started to reorganize the hospital so that conditions were starting to improve. However, winter had set in early and the battle-weary soldiers were suffering from the effects of extreme cold.

Plans for the wedding went ahead for the beginning of December, the banns were read and the village was in a frenzy of excitement.

The railway was progressing and had reached Canterbury and Julian had arranged for a new Bill to be presented to Parliament for the extension of his line beyond Dover through Sussex and further down the coast. The desire to possess his future bride became almost intolerable and each night in his own room he longed to visit her and had to discipline himself. Whether Alice expected any nocturnal intrusion to her bed he had no way of knowing, although she allowed him to embrace her and indeed had made no protest when his hand had caressed her bosom through the material of her dress. Further than that he dared not proceed, fearing to upset her obvious delight that his kisses provoked. The sooner they were married and desires fulfilled the better, but he realized that his obsession for her must be controlled.

The great day was fixed for the second week in December and there was much to do in and about the house. Julian very tactfully suggested that it would not be a bad idea to arrange for the exterior of the house to be refurbished and the gardens and paths including the driveway to have some attention.

'I know, my dear, I have been meaning to do all these things for longer than I care to admit, but it all costs so much and I keep putting it all off,' Alice said.

He smiled fondly at her.

'As this is going to be my home too, you really must allow me to do my share, and I am sure that I can find people who can do the whole job in no time. It's really the wrong time of year, but a touch of paint will make all the difference, and I'll get a gang to clean up the drive and spread some gravel, and perhaps cut the grass.' He was oblivious to the look of astonishment on her face. Clearly she was unused to having things done for her so forthrightly and in such a decisive manner.

'Come the spring we can have a proper job done, and I have a lot of ideas. What would you say to a conservatory facing south from the drawing room?'

Alice leaned over and kissed him on the lips. 'It all sounds marvellous, and I am not too proud to allow you to do this for me.' He interrupted her, returning her kiss.

'For me as well, my darling, it is our home and I want to do the best for both of us. I love planning and to see the results successfully achieved.'

They went on discussing plans for the house and gardens and their future life together. Perhaps a honeymoon in the spring, they would go abroad while the workmen were in the house. More staff would be needed both inside and outside. Clearly Julian intended to make his mark in the district and together with his viscountess become someone in the social world. But at the back of both their minds was the worry of her sons, with the fate of Jeremy in the balance.

Alice started to tell Julian about her younger son. How he was madly keen to join his father's old regiment, the 17th Lancers, and what a wonderful horseman he was, at one, as it were, with his steed. Like all the young men in the army he went off to the

Crimea full of thoughts of derring-do, but she learned from his letters how the euphoria quickly faded in the face of the dreadful conditions and the apparent lack of leadership in the field.

The workmen arrived one fine autumn day. New paint on the windows, doors and guttering soon transformed the old house. The gardens were trimmed and the long grass cut, shingle and gravel were delivered and raked onto the paths and drive. Then they moved indoors and soon new paint lightened the rooms. New curtains were ordered and hung and the extra staff that Julian had procured were soon busy cleaning, dusting and polishing the furniture. The house began to take on a new appearance and Alice went from room to room hardly daring to believe the reality of the transformation, happily admiring everything.

Soon the great day arrived, although their happiness was tempered by the absence of Alice's sons. At least she knew that Jeremy was alive and hopefully would be invalided home in due course. If only he could have been with them he could have given her away, as it was this was to be done by an old army friend of her first husband who was delighted to be asked, and to stand at her side in full uniform. Julian had asked Robert Stephenson, the famous engineer, to be his best man and now all was ready. The village folk were very excited and asked permission to decorate the church which was given with the full approval of the vicar who was just as excited as the rest.

It was a splendid country wedding. The little church was adorned with autumn flowers and foliage vying in colour with the splendid uniforms and gowns of the guests. The churchyard was crowded with the local people, and Julian's railwaymen had been given a day off and later crowded into a marquee set aside for them and the villagers to drink the health of the couple. Robert Stephenson gave a fine speech and a gala day was made more splendid by the gift of fine weather. The bride was radiant and looked quite beautiful, and Julian, very handsome in his morning suit, proudly gazed at her. He hardly dare believe she was now his wife and that the future could only be one of great happiness together.

At last the guests were gone and the servants had finished clearing up behind them. The evening was quiet in the old house, and so it was to bed, Alice with some trepidation and Julian barely controlling the excitement that filled his whole being.

He had kept his old bedroom but had bought a large double bed which was now installed in a newly decorated master bed chamber towards which he now led his bride. As he enfolded her in his arms she murmured, 'Darling I had not fully realized the full implications of marriage at my age. I suppose that I felt that it might be just a close companionship not the intimate relationship you obviously crave. But now I, too, want to lie in your arms and for you to make urgent love to me, but you may have to be very patient. It is indeed many years since I lay with a man, and I thought that those years had stifled my bodily needs. But you, my darling, have proved me wrong. And to think that had we not met I should never had thought differently.'

As she was speaking Julian had begun to unfasten the hooks on her gown that ran down her back almost to her buttocks, but now he stood back. 'Of course, my love, I am not thinking straight. Would you prefer to undress privately while I disrobe in my old room?

41

I realize now that this must be very traumatic for you although the urgency for me is overwhelming.'

'No, no, my sweet. I feel an abandonment I never knew that I possessed, quite a hoyden. I may be shy but am no innocent virgin. I long to caress your body too but you must be gentle with me, do not rush me into fulfilment.

He kissed her passionately and as the last hook yielded he slipped her gown from her shoulders. Petticoats and drawers followed rapidly. She had no need for stays or of other supports of that nature, and as he gazed boldly at her nakedness a deepening flush rose from her bosom and coloured her lovely features. He realized that she had the body of a woman thirty years younger with small but firm breasts, lithe thighs and hips carrying little surplus flesh.

'Quickly,' she breathed, 'it is my turn now.' And as he tore at his collar and cravat she, forgetting her previous shyness, busied herself with trouser buttons and underpants, until she, in her turn, could gaze at his manly nakedness. Feverishly she reached out to hold him, to touch his flesh, covering his chest with little kisses. Unable to wait longer, he picked her up bodily and drawing back the covers placed her tenderly on the bed and lay down beside her. Forgetting her plea for gentleness, in his lust to possess her, he thrust into her forcibly, breaching her tender flesh that had known no man for so long. A stifled cry and then she was gripping him and her moans soon became little cries of ecstacy.

Passion spent they lay quietly together saying little but murmuring endearments, but after a while she whispered in his ear and started to fondle him anew. She was like a young girl, completely abandoned in her desire for this man now her husband, and shyness was quite forgotten, her passion to make love equal to Julian's Once during the night she said something so quietly that he asked her to repeat it.

'I said is it not fortunate that I am past the age when you might make me pregnant!'

Days and nights followed showing no diminishment in their joy in each other. They strolled the gardens and planned what they would do. Julian was full of ideas. They would create a terrace, re-lay the lawns, create new herbaceous borders and plant an avenue of trees. Ideas were endless.

Then one morning a messenger arrived with a letter to say that Jeremy was being invalided home and should arrive before the end of January.

2

The sun was shining that brilliant October day but the sky was clouded with the smoke from countless Russian guns. All around cannon roared and the long valley echoed with their endless booming and the crackle of muskets and was filled with the holocaust of death. It would be a miracle if any survived who came within the range of the murderous fire-power of those guns. For this reason the intrepid cavalry under general Lord Cardigan were intent on capturing and silencing those very guns.

The valley was only a mile and a half long, and down it marched line after line of brilliantly uniformed men of the 8th Hussars, the 13th Light Bobs and the 17th Lancers. As they came within range of the guns some kept pushing ahead, no doubt thinking that their very speed would hasten the attack. They soon began to realize that they were doomed and wished to escape the hail of bullets and shells; very few were fortunate enough to do so.

When the advance was started a certain Captain Nolan had galloped up urging the Light Brigade to hasten the advance, but the guns ahead were making complete streets through the ranks and the smoke became so thick that the front lines could see very little, while the round shot, grape-shell and musketry mowed them down in whole groups.

Some of these gallant men, including Jeremy Lindley, actually reached the guns and dismounted to spike the cannon. Then came the awful realization that no back-up of infantry or indeed reinforcements from the Heavy Brigade had been sent to hold the position. And so those that had survived the charge had to remount and try to return down that valley of death and destruction. Jeremy saw his sergeant's head carried away by a roundshot, but the body remained upright in the saddle with lance still levelled. He saw troopers sitting on the ground propped up against fallen horses staring unbelieving where but a moment before their legs had supported them but were now ragged bloody stumps.

Now the Russian Cossacks were amongst the retreat spearing the wounded helpless men, those who but a short while ago, in their richly adorned uniforms were advancing with sabres and lances levelled, and were now soaked in blood, stumbling back to the British lines as best they could. Some with shattered limbs, others with dreadful head-wounds, some walking holding on to a stirrup or still astride wounded horses.

To Jeremy Lindley came the realization that it was hopeless staying with the captured guns. Turning his horse's head he started back to safety. He had lost sight of Wilson, his orderly, some time before and now he found himself with others he knew who had the same thought, to escape from this hellish carnage. A Russian charged at him and Jeremy struck hard at his head but he only succeeded in breaking his sabre at the hilt when it struck the enemy's helmet. Just then his left arm received a hit and the bone shattered. Holding the broken limb as best he could

45

across his knee he held the reins in his teeth. It was now every man for himself and he pushed his horse into a gallop and eventually passed through a line of Polish lancers who had ranked across the line of retreat preventing the Cossacks further pursuit.

Feeling faint now from loss of blood he continued to urge his horse forward to escape the hail of fire which continued to harass the retreat. Eventually he stopped. Someone was holding his gallant horse, whose flanks were heaving from its exertions and eyes wide from fright. Someone else held a flask of rum to his lips whilst others lifted him from the saddle and placed him on a stretcher and carried him to the rear. He saw wounded horses standing forlornly awaiting succour but only to be shot putting them out of their misery. Surgeons were examining the wounded, amputating limbs in the open air, and sewing up dreadful sabre cuts and lance wounds. As the daylight faded the women came out to look for the bodies of their loved ones and to bring them in. There was blood everywhere amongst sawn off legs and arms; to Jeremy it was a scene from hell!

He was taken to a dressing station where a surgeon examined his shattered arm. He was preparing to amputate at the shoulder when Jeremy begged him to delay. The surgeon shrugged and had a further look. 'All right, old fellow, it ought to come off but I'll strap it up as best as I can and sew up the artery. Perhaps if we can stop the bleeding we can have another look tomorrow.' He gave him a draught of laudanum and Jeremy soon became drowsy.

The next day he was taken to the shore with others also badly wounded and helped into a boat. The vast Turkish barracks at Scutari on the mainland the other side of the Black Sea had been taken over as a hospital and convoys of small boats were being used to convey the wounded across the water. Fortunately the sea was calm and the short voyage was uneventful.

The hospital was immense, having two floors set around a central parade ground, and parts were in a shocking state. There was accommodation for some one thousand beds including use of the corridors. The Turkish idea of beds was just low wooden shelves set around the walls, which were filthy and infested with rats. The officers fared little better than the enlisted men although they were kept separate and probably enjoyed somewhat better attention. The men were originally tended by male orderlies as no suitable women could be found.

However a gradual change for the better had started that autumn when that very intrepid lady, Florence Nightingale, arrived on the scene with the first of her volunteer nurses. She brought order out of chaos and was ruthless in her demands for better conditions and the supply of medicines and bandages. Soon more help arrived from various institutions, Sisters of Mercy, various charities and more importantly from the organization of the Sellonites, an order of mercy formed by Miss Priscilla Sellon. It was only these latter out of the original party of volunteer lady nurses who were to work through the whole of that terrible winter, and who under Miss Nightingale achieved some sort of order from the appalling conditions prevalent in the Crimean hospitals.

Jeremy's senses slowly returned, and apart from the throbbing of the injured flesh the pain was bearable. He gazed up into the face of the nurse seeing only an angel of mercy, her eyes full of understanding and sympathy. In reality it was rather

47

a plain face but with good features, especially her eyes which were of the deepest blue. When she stood up, her bandaging finished, he saw that she was tall and slim, but the drab uniform disguised her figure and belied her beauty. In his present state her caring look was all that interested him.

She brought him a drink of lime water, helping him to drink. 'You should try and sleep now, maybe later you will be able to eat something.'

'Tell me your name please. I should like to know so that perhaps I can dream of you and my mind can be at peace and forget this awful day.' He shuddered as the scenes from that dreadful afternoon filled his thoughts. The holocaust of death, the cacophany of cannon and the shrieking of horses and men alike. The blood, always the blood everywhere.

'Fiona, Fiona Fortescue,' she brushed away the tears that threatened to blur her vision as she sensed his thoughts. No man should have to endure that these brave men has been ordered to do. This war, the killing and maiming of such gallant men, was wicked. This hospital was full to overflowing with the remnants of fine soldiers. Although, since the arrival of Miss Nightingale, conditions had vastly improved. But there was so much room for more to ease their suffering. She knew that the vast majority would die, generally from shock, but also from their horrendous wounds and the gangrene that inevitably followed. And many would succumb to cholera and typhus which were rife in the hospital. 'Try and sleep now.' She wiped his sweaty brow with a damp cloth. 'I'll be back from time to time but I have so many patients to see.'

'Of course Fiona. You are a veritable angel. I think that I shall be able to sleep now.' In fact his eyes were drooping. He was so tired; maybe the rum he had been given on top of the laudanum was having the desired effect. Fiona stayed for a moment longer and then as he slept she left him to continue her ministrations elsewhere. 'Dear God,' she thought, 'save these brave men and let this dreadful war be over soon, very soon.'

All that night through to first light the following morning casualties were still being brought in from the clearing station on the battlefield. Some might live, given good nursing, but most would die in the following day or two; others might linger on more dead than alive.

Jeremy seemed more rested when Fiona visited him next day although he was running a slight fever, which she assured him was quite normal after the gruelling operation on his arm. She removed the bandage, washing the wound thoroughly. It was much inflamed around the stitches, but seemed to be draining satisfactorily. She checked the splints and rebound it tightly. 'I will try and do this again during the day. Try to keep it still which will give the flesh a chance to heal. The bone will come together given time, but I doubt that you will ever be able to use it satisfactorily as the tendons are badly damaged. It is, perhaps, fortunate that it is your left arm.'

After she had left him he felt well enough to take stock of his surroundings. The couches were all occupied and he caught sight of some he knew, but few were in any state to talk and lay semi-conscious with bloodied bandages covering the dreadful stumps where legs and arms had been so short a time before. Some had their heads swathed in cloths covering shocking wounds from sabre slash. He managed to eat a little when next she visited him with an orderly, who made out a diet for him. This was written out on a card and, as with every patient, pinned above his bed.

It was not for another day or two that he was able to converse for any length of time with Fiona, his fever having gone, and it was while she was bathing him with little embarrassment that he asked her about herself. She told him that she was from the Sellonite Sisters of Mercy, so called because their founder was a Miss Priscilla Sellon, who had volunteered to send some of her ladies to help Miss Nightingale. Fiona was of gentle breeding and had found her vocation in nursing the sick and destitute in England. Many of her class had failed to find romance and marriage and had subsequently devoted their lives to caring for others.

Jeremy surmised that she was far from unmarriageable, and thought that although somewhat plain, and perhaps unexciting for most men's taste, would nevertheless make an excellent wife and might well meet someone one day to whom she could devote her life. In fact the more he saw of her he realized that she indeed possessed hidden depths of which she might be unaware. Many patients were prone to think that they were in love with their nurses who looked after them with tenderness and caring, who soothed their feverish brows and who seemed to be veritable angels. Jeremy, although he was improving daily with as yet no sign of further infection, was not immune to the effect Fiona had upon him. Her quiet efficiency and readiness to talk with him made up for her plain looks, and he saw in her more than was on the surface and he began to enjoy the more intimate touches her nursing necessitated.

As his health improved he was able to look around him and take in more of his surroundings, seeing them for what they were and the appalling conditions under which the nurses had to cope. He soon found out that there was no operating theatre as such and the wounded were operated upon where they lay, be it wards or in the corridors. Chloroform was in short supply and only used in extreme cases. Usually it was a case of being given rum and tightly strapped down to prevent movement and struggling. This, of course, resulted in further shock and was probably the reason for so many unnecessary deaths. Another reason was the lack of hygiene which became inevitable with the unending streams of casualties.

Some of the wards were very delapidated inasmuch that with heavy rain the roof leaked so that sometimes the floors were awash. Added to this was the ghastly state of the latrines. These were of the Turkish 'squatting' variety, where the drains discharged straight into the sea with no water trap or flushing system. This resulted in a continuous smell which emanated through the wards. To try and combat this foul stench soldiers were wont to try and block the drains in an attempt to stifle it, with the result that at high tide the wards flooded and conditions worsened. In fact more than another year was to pass before new latrines with proper systems were installed, by which time, of course, it was too late for many of the patients. Jeremy began to wonder how any could survive when he saw so many with bowel infections. It was, in fact, a nightmare situation and he had nothing but admiration for the doctors and nurses, most of whom had not been reared for or taught to cope with these conditions.

For those who were recovering, or not too direly ill, another noxious smell pervading the hospital attracted their increasing awareness of their

51

surroundings. One day he asked Fiona what it could be, but she seemed reluctant to discuss it. But when he persisted she eventually disclosed the alarming reason for it. Apparently the burial grounds were adjacent to the hospital which in itself was a demoralizing state of affairs. But added to this was the ghastly manner of Turkish burial, where the corpses were buried neither deeply or even securely, encouraging the ever-present rats and other vermin, so that when the wind was in the wrong direction the smell of putrefaction wafted through the wards. Knowledge of this did little for the morale of the patients.

Added to all this were the rats themselves which seemed everywhere and the dirt and unsavoury clothing were harbouring lice. When Miss Nightingale first came to the hospital she soon embarked on a system for using lysol freely, and burning the infected clothing. It was not long however before there was a shortage of shirts for the men so that before the dead were buried their shirts were removed for use by the living and sacking used on the bodies instead. There was also an inadequate system of water supply only available at one or two places and not fed to the wards themselves.

Jeremy has lost all sense of the passing days and it was only when the chaplain brought communion to the whole ward, the living and dying alike, that he realized that it was Christmas. There was no sign of any festivities, which in any case would have been out of place with so many grievously wounded.

One day Fiona failed to visit him, leaving him disappointed but it was only after a further two days that her absence began to worry him, and on asking, was told that she was sick and confined to bed in the nurses' quarters which were in one of the towers. He began to worry about her and sought permission to visit her which was refused. However he persevered, and ultimately he was escorted to her room by another nurse.

Fiona, he learned, had been feeling unwell for some days, but she had attributed it to the unwholesome atmosphere of the hospital and the lack of fresh air. One morning she had been unable to rise and the doctor had been to visit her. She had wondered whether she had succumbed to cholera which was rife in the hospital and very contagious. Jeremy was distraught to see her looking so ill and stayed for a while holding her hand encouraging her as best he could.

She continued in this state for another week or so feeling very weak and ill so as not to care what was happening around her and later she learned that she had been expected to die. Miss Nightingale herself looked after her and she steadily began to recover, gaining strength all the time. She began to worry that she would be sent home and was loath to leave her beloved patients, and these fears were to be realized in the weeks ahead.

During this time the hospital was shaken by an earthquake. The wards rocked and everyone feared the worst and that the roof would collapse and bury them all. Great fear ensued and there was a stampede by those that could walk to get outside, some even leaping from the windows. The shaking continued for a while and even the bravest in battle were crying out in fear. Jeremy was as scared as any and joined the rush to evacuate the building, until upon reaching the open air his self-discipline returned and he set about calming the others, calling upon them to remember their training and bear themselves as the disciplined soldiers that they were. Gradually his good sense prevailed and somewhat shame-facedly their calm was restored.

It was not long after this that together with several others Jeremy was informed that he was to be evacuated and sent home. Only too glad to leave this ghastly place, it was with mixed feelings that he was to say farewell to the many friends he had made and known in battle. So many had gone, men of his own troop and fellow officers and non-commissioned ranks. However, when he learned that Fiona and another nurse were also being sent home with them, he was over the moon with delight.

Her worst fears had been realized. She was convalescing well and able to travel, but was loath to leave the wounded whom she had nursed with such devotion. This had been, she thought, ordained from the first; being the destiny for which she had always wished, and the culmination of her hard and difficult training. She felt somewhat better, however, when Miss Nightingale explained to her that the men who were being sent home had to be accompanied by nurses and those that were fit could hardly be spared. Indeed many of the soldiers would need constant care on the long sea-voyage. Thus Fiona's reluctance to leave was tempered by this necessity and the need for her to continue her work.

The great day came when Jeremy stood on the quayside with the others and a minimum of luggage awaiting transport to the steamship that lay at anchor offshore. They steamed past Constantinople, and on looking back could see the lights of the hospital glimmering through the dusk, at which point their thoughts returned to those poor fellows left behind in their misery, and the work of the doctors and nurses who would continue their ministrations in that doleful place.

The ship was French, one of the first stern screw vessels to be built, but carried sails on two masts in addition to her engine. The great majority of the passengers were French wounded and there were French nurses attending them. For Jeremy it might have been a pleasant voyage but for the evident suffering of some of the poor invalid soldiers, and several died and had to be buried at sea. Some lay on deck too ill to be taken below, while those that were recovering helped to look after them.

Fortunately the Mediterranean was calm and quite beautiful. Passing through the Straits of Messina they caught sight of Mount Etna, and two days later they reached Marseilles where they stopped to take on coal for the engine. That evening, while Jeremy stood on deck by the rail looking out at the lights of the city, he sensed the approach of a nurse who silently came and stood beside him. Seeing that it was Fiona, who had replaced her nurse's cap with a scarf, he felt very happy that she should seek his company. Presently she reached out and gently laid her hand on his injured arm, which was still tightly splinted.

'How does it feel, Jeremy, have you still much pain?' This was the first time that they had been alone together. He turned towards her, surprised that she had used his first name. He was only slightly taller than she as she moved to face him, and he saw her calmly composed features set in lines of great compassion. She was not by any means a beautiful woman, but Jeremy realized that it was her brilliant blue eyes that redeemed her otherwise severe expression. Those eyes were now directed towards him without guile and a complete absence of shyness as might have been the case with most young women alone aboard ship with a handsome soldier.

'Tell me about yourself, Jeremy. Have you a family? Have you been a soldier long?' And so they talked quietly together. He told her of his home in Kent. How he had followed his father, who had died when quite young, into his old regiment. No, he had not married, the army was his life and his great love was for horses. He told her of his mother who, he hesitantly admitted, was a peeress although now something of a recluse since his elder brother was institutionalized following a riding accident.

Then it was her turn. Gently he encouraged her to talk about herself. That she had lost both her parents before she was twenty years old and left to fend for herself with very little money. She had never had the opportunity of meeting any man in whom she might have found some mutual attraction, so she had put aside any thought of marriage. Then one day a friend had introduced her to Priscilla Sellon and from then on her outlook on life took on a new meaning, nursing the sick and poor, bringing succour and help to the needy. Miss Sellon, like Florence Nightingale, was a special kind of person, dedicated to her work and banding a company of special ladies to her own dedicated way of life. This had been Fiona's vocation for the last three years, and although no nun, she had no interest in a social life or in the opposite sex.

Jeremy listened without interrupting, and as Fiona talked she seemed to lose her shyness and became animated as she enthused about the joy her dedicated way of life brought to her, and a faint flush brought a bloom to her cheeks. He could not but contemplate what a transformation there would be in this girl should her apparel be more feminine and reveal more of her figure, of which so little could be seen under her dreadful clothes. He guessed there was something of a beautiful body which the girl was intent on hiding so that she could shut herself off from the world she had eschewed. He changed his position so that he faced her and quietly reached out with his good arm and gently held her hand. At first the contact of their flesh made her stiffen but she gradually relaxed as he tentatively squeezed her fingers, and then, to his delight, she responded by placing her other hand over his.

Jeremy made no attempt at further presumption, and they stayed like that while she continued to tell him about herself.

'What of your plans when you get back to England? You will find your life rather humdrum after Scutari, although a little more pleasant I should think,' he said.

'Oh, I will see Miss Sellon in due course. No doubt she will have further plans for me. But you are quite right, it will seem odd to go back to my old life and I shall miss my poor soldiers. Although so many died it was a wonderful thing when we were able to save just a few and help them to recover from that awful war. It's something that I shall always carry with me, that I was allowed to alleviate some of the suffering.'

'Yes Fiona. I owe you my arm you know. If it had not been for you I would have lost it, and maybe I would not be here standing beside you.' A wonderful idea crossed his mind, and what a change it might make to the girl's outlook. She should not be allowed to shut herself away so strictly from life, and he was sure she had so much more to offer, given a chance.

'Fiona, I know this may sound silly to you, but why

don't you come and stay at my home for a short holiday. God knows you need one. You are still not completely recovered from your malaise and neither am I. My arm still needs a lot of attention, and who knows with your help I might fully regain the use of it. I know that my mother would love to meet you and the country life will put colour in your cheeks, and you will enjoy the peace and quiet of our home. Why don't we go and see Miss Sellon together and discuss it with her. I am sure she will agree.'

'Oh, Jeremy, that would be nice.' Her voice became quite animated. 'But I ought to continue my work, there are so many poor and needy to look after, and Miss Sellon is so short-handed, I expect she will have other plans for me. But the thought of a holiday away from all that we have been through is a wonderful prospect.' She grasped his hand more tightly. 'Thank you my dear, it's such a kind suggestion and I really do appreciate it.'

'That is settled then.' Jeremy decided to brook no further argument. 'We will see Miss Sellon when we get back. Unless of course by the end of this long voyage you are heartily sick of the sight of me and will not want my company longer.'

'I should think that highly unlikely, my dear, for I find your company most reassuring. I am much happier than when we left, for I was very sad to leave my work at the hospital and did not really wish to go home. The thought of resuming a rather dreary life would have been such an anti-climax after all the excitements and dramas of Scutari. But your suggestion and kind invitation gives me something to look forward to. And now, my dear, I think I will go below and find my bunk for I am quite sleepy.'

Towards evening the next day they entered the Bay

of Biscay, and true to its reputation the weather worsened and towards midnight a full storm was raging, the huge seas sweeping over the exposed decks and the bows of the ship more often under the water than above it. The skylights were battened down and covered so that little air penetrated below and the atmosphere soon became fetid and foul. Most of the invalids soon became sea-sick and the nurses themselves were soon prostrate and panic-stricken. Around two o'clock in the morning there was a tremendous crash and all thought that the ship was foundering and everyone became hysterical until one of the ship's officers appeared to reassure them and to tell them that the ship had slowed down to avoid the tremendous battering of the waves, but that all was well.

Towards dawn the sea quietened down and a few intrepid nurses ventured on deck, being very careful to avoid being swept over the side as the motion was far from steady, and the ship seemed to be riding over the waves rather than cutting through them. They were told that such was the force of the storm that the ship's prow had been buckled and many fittings washed away. Although the wind rose again that night it was not as fierce as before, and by now they had become used to the motion and felt more reassured. The following day the ship was able to increase speed so that in no time they were in the English Channel. Soon, to the excitement of all who could struggle on deck, they saw the white cliffs of Dover in the distance.

That afternoon they berthed at Folkestone where there were crowds waiting on the quayside to welcome them together with horse-drawn ambulances and conveyances of every kind. Soon doctors came on board to check the wounded and sick, and there was tremendous excitement prevailing everywhere. Large banners were apparent everywhere proclaiming 'WELCOME HOME TO OUR BRAVE SOLDIERS'. Jeremy kept close to Fiona unwilling to lose her in the throng. He saw a middle-aged smartly dressed woman pushing her way determinedly towards them. Fiona saw her at the same moment and waved frantically.

'It's Miss Sellon, Jeremy, oh how marvellous,' and with a happy cry of 'Priscilla', flung her arms about the newcomer, hugging her.

Disentangling herself after a moment she introduced Jeremy.

'This is Captain Jeremy Lindley, of the 17th Lancers, and lately of Scutari hospital, and my favourite patient!' A flush suffused her cheeks as she realized what she had said, but Jeremy, covering her embarrassment, quickly interrupted.

'And you are Priscilla Sellon, about whom I have heard so much, and whose nurses have done and still are doing such marvellous work. If it had not been for Fiona this arm would have found a permanent home in the ground.' He smiled as he patted the injured limb and shook her hand. They chatted for a while longer and then Miss Sellon told them she had a carriage waiting and invited Jeremy to share it.

They were about to move away when an officer in resplendent uniform approached.

'Jeremy Lindley aren't you? My dear fellow,' he went on as Jeremy acknowledged him with a smart salute, 'I really am delighted to see you'. He glanced at the splinted arm. 'More or less in one piece at any rate. You are one of the more fortunate, I hear, all quite tragic I believe. But the stories of the Charge of

the Light Brigade have become something of an epic.'
Jeremy introduced him.

'Major Fellowes, this is Miss Fortescue who nursed
me, and Miss Sellon who is responsible for organizing
her gallant band of nurses.'

The major saluted. 'Your servant, ladies.' Turning
back to Jeremy he asked him his plans for conva-
lescence.

'Home for me, sir, with your permission of course,
and I have asked Miss Fortescue to come and stay
with me and look after me at the same time.' Turning
to Miss Sellon, he said, 'I hope that meets with your
approval too, ma'am. Actually, although she has not
as yet told you, Fiona has been quite ill too. I suspect
that she could do with a change and fresh air in the
country would do her the power of good.'

'That would be most kind of you, Captain Lindley.
I had no idea you had been sick, Fiona, of course you
must take a holiday and when you feel yourself again
come and see me. I fear there is so much work to do
still, there always is!'

3

Julian gazed through the window at the change he had brought about at Brush Hall. The gardens had been transformed from their previous state of neglect, and he was proud of what he and Alice had done in so short a time. It was early summer and everywhere showed the promise of new growth and instilled in him a deep contentment. He and Alice had become lovers in every sense of the word, and he marvelled at the change that had come over his life in so short a time. His railway progressed, he had won the mail contract in spite of intense opposition and his Bill for the extension along the south coast was receiving favourable attention in parliament.

Added to this was Allice's great happiness when her son had arrived unexpectedly with the charming Fiona Fortescue. They had learned that Jeremy was being invalided home but had heard nothing further until they arrived unheralded. A pity really for had they known in advance Julian could have arranged a special train to bring home Alice's soldier son in style. No matter, Alice was ecstatic and Julian was quite taken by his step-son. He seemed a fine fellow, and his reaction to his mother's romance and marriage was one of apparent pleasure, and he could see for himself his mother's new found happiness and contentment.

Although reluctant at first to talk about the battle, the peace and quiet of his home began to relax him and he was able to be more detached from his memories of the carnage and slaughter. Julian told him that the epic charge was the main topic of conversation everywhere, and stories, some exaggerated and probably coloured by imagination, were rife.

Jeremy, although somewhat restrained when telling of his own part in the battle, was able to describe incidents as he remembered them. How Lord Cardigan had been at the forefront of the charge and first to reach the Russian guns.

'If only Lord Raglan, the commander-in-chief, had ordered the Heavy Brigade forward we would have won the day. The guns would have been taken and the enemy routed. But there were no reinforcements and so no other option but to retreat and leave the guns. And so many fine men, the flower of our cavalry, perished, as many in retreat as in the advance.' He was silent for a moment as were his listeners. 'I heard that out of nearly six hundred at Balaclava only one hundred and ninety five returned, and over five hundred horses were lost one way of another. All that in just over half an hour.'

His mother involuntarily stretched out her arm to him. 'Thank God that you were spared, my darling, it must have been a miracle that you survived. That any survived from what you have described. Oh those poor young men! I have heard that Alfred Lord Tennyson is to write a patriotic ballad about the charge.'

Jeremy frowned. 'How can he possibly write about that when he wasn't there? He cannot have the

63

slightest inkling of that dreadful carnage, whole men suddenly becoming "half-men" with no legs or with shattered arms, just bloodied stumps!'

Julian interposed. 'Epic battle or no, I think we should try and allow Jeremy to forget this nightmare, what do you think?' He turned to Fiona but before she could reply, he went on, 'I understand that Miss Nightingale was a veritable martinet. That she brooked no argument with the army officials.'

'She was marvellous,' Fiona replied. 'Our little band of nurses arrived at Scutari with her. There was absolute chaos when we first got there, very few medicines, shortage of bandages and blankets. She very quickly got things organized, and as you say she stood no nonsense from the doctors in charge, and the hospital director was told exactly what was wanted, and she got it. That so many wounded survived was in great part due to her.'

'And to you and your band of nurses, bless you all,' Jeremy added.

Neither Jeremy or Fiona had managed to bring many clothes with them. Jeremy, coming straight from the battle to hospital with his uniform in tatters, had managed to borrow what he could. Fiona had been instructed to take very little and had no 'party' clothes only a change of uniform, and was embarrassed that the small amount of money she had would not enable her to rectify this. Alice intuitively guessed how things were, and, after discussing the problem with Julian, decided to take the girl in hand.

'We will go up to London on one of Julian's trains, you will both enjoy the experience. It is so comfortable and quick, and dear Julian will be so proud to show you his achievements. I was quite scared the first time I travelled with him, we seemed to go so fast with the countryside seeming to flash past the windows and the engine snorting with clouds of smoke like some prehistoric monster.'

'But you soon got used to it, didn't you my dear?' Julian interrupted, smiling.

'Oh yes indeed, and we were in London in no time at all, with no effort involved, and so comfortable in the beautifully upholstered seats. Mind you, that was in the first class carriage of course. I dare say the workers' carriages are not so well furbished.'

Later, when Alice was alone with her husband, she again broached the subject of Fiona's finances, and it was agreed that a wardrobe should be purchased in keeping with the girl's social position and that it should be their contribution and a thanksgiving for the part Fiona had played in bringing succour to the many wounded soldiers and especially in the case of Jeremy whom she had brought home safe and almost sound.

And so a week or two later the journey was made, the train to London was stopped at the Brush Halt where a carriage had been reserved for them. Although Jeremy had seen the trains in operation before he had never travelled on one, and both he and Fiona began to enjoy the new experience. Julian had even arranged for a picnic to be served, and so it was a happy little party that arrived at the great smoky terminus in the south of the capital city.

Carriages were waiting and while Jeremy went off to the Strand where he intended to visit his military tailor, Alice took Fiona off to Libertys where they were soon surrounded by shop assistants with a variety of dresses and suits suitable for all occasions. The girl was visibly embarrassed but her protests were swept aside and eventually she gave in and began to enjoy herself and all the attention that she was receiving. While all this was going on Julian took himself off, content to let Alice take charge, to make several business calls, and agreeing to pick up the ladies later.

Finally, with some reluctance on Fiona's part, Alice was satisfied with their selection which not only included dresses and costumes, but underwear and night attire, as well as footwear and stockings. The girl was quite overwhelmed, as everything was carefully packed into a large trunk, but wisely decided to accept this munificent gift in good grace.

Just as they were about to leave, a messenger boy arrived on his bicycle with a note from Jeremy. In it he explained that he had been joined at his tailor by a staff officer from his regiment on the same errand as himself, who was an old friend and comrade. It appeared that he knew all about Jeremy's wounds and had considered it expedient that he should have his arm checked by no less than Doctor Smith, who was the director general of the Army Medical Department, and whom his friend knew well. He would arrange an appointment for the following day. This being so Jeremy wrote that he would be staying overnight at the Army and Navy club, and would hopefully be able to return to Brush in a day or two depending on Doctor Smith's recommendations for future treatment, should any prove necessary. He was hopeful that the splints would no longer be needed. This seemed splendid news and Alice was thankful that her son would be in good hands.

That evening, back at Brush Hall, Alice decided that Fiona should wear one of her new dresses to show herself off before Julian. When he entered the drawing room and saw her he could hardly credit the transformation. Gone was the rather dowdy and somewhat plain girl, and he could only gape at the tall, slim woman in her place. The dress she wore accentuated the lovely lines of her body which had hitherto been hidden. Slim she might be but she had small but perfect thrusting breasts above a seemingly non-existent stomach and small rounded hips, and he could only imagine the well formed thighs and long tapering legs hidden beneath her dress.

Julian experienced a sudden overwhelming desire to possess her. He doubted whether she had ever had a man in her life and certainly never in her bed. Undoubtedly she was a virgin and probably had never experienced sexual feelings for any man, but she aroused in him the basest feelings of lust which for a moment clouded his reason. In some intuitive way Fiona seemed to sense what was passing through his mind, and a slow hot flush began to colour her neck and face, but she was somehow powerless to avoid looking at him.

Alice, however, seeing the girl blush, mistakenly thought that it was caused by shyness, unused as she had been to showing herself off in front of Julian in her lovely new dress, and so was quite unaware of the feelings the girl had stimulated in her husband. The incident was only momentary and with a great effort Julian banished his awareness of his sexual attraction and took great pains to speak normally to Alice.

'She looks lovely in that dress, dear, you have both been very clever in your choice and it suits her admirably.' Jokingly he added, 'Am not I the most fortunate of men to be surrounded by two such lovely ladies.'

Throughout the evening he made every effort to be his normal self and forebore to allow his glance to linger on the girl longer than was normal, but whenever he did happen to catch her eye she shyly looked away, and he realized with something of a shock that Fiona was well aware of what had occurred and had not the experience in how to react. But he knew that any overt action on his part would frighten the girl, and she would not dare stay on at Brush, and that was the last thing he wanted to happen. He was at a loss to understand his feelings. He was in love with Alice and was as happy as any man could be; he had fulfilled everything he had wanted, but here was a girl whose sudden physical attraction could jeopardize everything and could well ruin his happy marriage. And yet he could not banish the thoughts from his mind of the conquest of this girl's virginity. The surrender of her innocence could only stimulate his further desire for her. He had to discipline himself, temper this carnal desire, which was only conceived in the last hour or two, and thrust it aside. It was a product of middle age, he admitted wryly to himself, and not be considered further.

Fiona's mind was in turmoil. That night, as she lay in bed, she tried to rationalize her feelings. Julian had stirred some latent desire in her body which she had never been aware of before. She had never ever considered her body to be desirable to men, but as she saw again his eyes roving over her body, which she now realized had revealed itself by the clinging shape of her new gown, the hot flush betrayed her innermost feelings, and the strongest of the age-old emotions seemed to control her limbs. She found it difficult not to succumb to the intimate sensations which threatened to overwhelm her.

She was not ignorant of the form of the male body nor of its functions, but the patients she had nursed so caringly had always been in a flaccid state and raised no curiosity in her, or caused any sexual feelings. Her emotions towards them were of pity and the need to help them. Her adult life had never brought her into contact intimate enough to arouse any feelings toward the opposite sex. What she was experiencing now was completely alien to a hitherto innocent existence. In her innermost mind she felt an excitement that she endeavoured vainly to quell, and in the end gave up the effort and allowed her body to indulge the wonderful sensations that it craved, and in her imagination allowed herself the fantasy of fulfulment, imagining this man's hands caressing her limbs in the most shameful manner. Finally she slept a dreamless sleep, but in the morning, remembering her fantasies, she felt ashamed at her weakness and the carnal thoughts that had filled her mind. She determined to banish any further lustful imaginings. But how? It was the gown that had betrayed her. Should she revert to her dowdy dress? But then Alice, who had been so generous and kind, would be dreadfully hurt and at a loss to understand, and she would hate this to happen. She realized that she ought to make some excuse and return to her work in London, but she had to admit to herself that up to now she had been tremendously happy at Brush, and had fallen into the habit of enjoying this new life.

But later that morning Alice was to make a suggestion which would alter her thinking, and defer any further decision she might have to make. The previous night while Fiona had been agonizing in her fantasies, Alice, lying beside her husband, began to talk about her elder son Gerald, who was in the mental institution at nearby Chartham.

Their gentle love making was not as prolonged as

was usual and Julian realized that her thoughts had drifted away from their mutual endearments, and asked her if anything was the matter.

'I am so sorry, my darling, but I have been so happy these last few months and now I am ashamed to realize that I had spared no thoughts for Gerald, and now I am filled with remorse.' Julian was silent guessing that she had more to say, and waited for her to continue.

'I have suddenly had an idea. Something that will salve my guilty conscience over the lack of consideration for my elder son. I am afraid that I have rather allowed matters to look after themselves and not paid enough attention to his future welfare.'

'I gather that there is no change in his condition, nor has there been for several months,' Julian interrupted.

'No, poor boy. He is in quite a stable condition, his physical health seems to be fair, but his mind is a complete blank, and has been ever since that tragic accident. He recognizes the people who look after him and can communicate with them, and to some extent do things for himself probably more from habit than intuition, and they tell me he is quite harmless and good natured. But no more than that.'

The glimmering of an idea began to manifest itself to Julian, but he waited to see what Alice had in mind and wondered whether she was thinking along the same lines as himself. He was soon proved right, and he smiled to himself as Alice continued.

'I thought . . . oh dear I hope I am not presuming on your generosity darling but . . . I was wondering why we cannot have him home. I mean he is quite harmless but needs much care and nursing. And,' the words came out quickly, 'after all we have a trained

70

nurse already here, if Fiona would only agree. She is becoming embarrassed by her financial state, and worried by her reliance on our generosity. I am sure that she will soon think it necessary to go back to London to earn her keep. Oh Julian, what do you think? I know it will mean much forebearance on your part, but it would be lovely to make this effort.' Her voice trailed away and she watched Julian's expression as anxiously she waited to see what his reaction to this idea would be.

'As soon as you mentioned the matter the same idea occurred to me. You see great minds think alike,' he added jocularly. 'I think it might be well worth seeing if Fiona will agree, at any rate for a while to see how matters progress. And I agree with you that she might welcome the idea of earning some money. I am sure that we could reach some satisfactory arrangement with her. Also it would be much better if Gerald can begin to recognize his own home and come to know his mother again.'

Alice was quite overcome and flung herself into Julian's arms quite forgetting her habitual reserve. 'Oh you are a wonderful man and so good to me. We must put it to Fiona, and see what she thinks about it. Oh, you have made me so happy, and it will be wonderful to be able to help Gerald.'

Julian was glad to be able to bring such happiness to his wife although he realized that he would do anything in order to prevent Fiona leaving Brush. He had determined to discipline his feelings towards the girl, but he also knew that he would be loath to see her leave, and in spite of himself a feeling of desire in his loins manifested itself to be quickly banished before it should be noticed by Alice.

'We had better have a chat with Fiona and find out

71

what she thinks, and whatever salary we offer her must be realistic. I do not suppose that looking after Gerald will be easy and will call for a degree of unselfishness but that I am sure she possesses having done what she did at Scutari. The question is whether she will think her duty lies further afield with Miss Sellon and the many poor and needy that need looking after so desperately. But we can but see.'

When they later put the idea to Fiona, she was at first very much in two minds whether to accept their very generous offer. She had, of course, heard about Gerald although the subject had rarely been mentioned, and she had felt desperately sorry for Alice that her eldest son should have been so cruelly struck down in the riding accident. She loved being at Brush, it was such a completely different way of life to that which she had been accustomed. She knew that she ought to leave and never see Julian again, for his very presence continued to effect her willpower which seemed unable to conquer her weak body and the heady desire he imbued in her. She also supposed she might be letting down Miss Sellon, although she had told her she should stay at Brush for a while. In the end she decided to compromise and stay a while longer and write to Miss Sellon explaining the situation. Although this might well prove dangerous as far as Julian was concerned, her body literally tingled at the thought of his continued nearness, and what might well happen at any time.

The next move would be a visit to Chartham institution which was always somewhat traumatic. For to see so many mentally sick men and women was very depressing and Alice had always come away distraught not only because of Gerald but with a sadness for the other patients.

And so Fiona wrote to Miss Sellon and Alice arranged to see the director of the institution the following week when Fiona had received a reply to her letter. This came quite soon. Miss Sellon approved the idea for a limited duration but hoped that Fiona would not forget her vocation to help the poor and sick, and that she would hope to see the girl again in the new year. To keep the lady 'sweet' as Julian put it, he decided to send her a donation which should be used for the benefit of her order.

'If nothing else,' he said, 'that should ease our conscience!'

The interview at Chartham went off more easily than Alice had dared expect. They were both sounded out thoroughly on the nursing care and attention Gerald might expect. The director stressed that Gerald would need constant supervision. His new surroundings would be strange to him as would his mother and Julian. They would need great patience and fortitude and should expect no immediate improvement. He assured them that Gerald was not violent in any way.

As they listened to him in silence, Alice was thinking that on the one hand how marvellous it would be to have her eldest son with her again, to mother him and cosset his enfeebled mind. But on the other she hoped they were not making a mistake. Would they be able to cope with the difficulties that were bound to arise realizing that Gerald would be unable to fend for himself in most things? Of course the idea would never have arisen had not Fiona, with all her nursing experience, been with them.

As if sensing what she was thinking, the doctor paused and then continued, 'If I might make a suggestion. Supposing I let you have the male orderly, whom your son knows, to stay with you for a few days. At least until Gerald has got used to his new surroundings. You have to realize, although it was his own home, he will not remember it, at least not at first. With this help it will not be so completely strange, and your Miss Fortescue can pick up the routine and continue the same sequence of nursing, so that there need be no break in what he has been accustomed to. How would that suit you?'

'That would be most considerate of you doctor,' Julian glanced at his wife who nodded vigorously. 'I am sure that Miss Fortescue would be very happy to concur.' They talked a while about medication, diet and much else that would be necessary in Gerald's nursing.

'Right, I think that covers everything. Should you have any queries or should we think of anything else we can keep in touch. Now let me see. You will have to prepare his rooms and get everything ready, and I think that we, here, should try and put his mind at rest that he will be leaving what, after all, has been his home for a long time; suppose we say in two weeks time I will arrange for Gerald and the orderly to be brought to Brush Hall.'

Meanwhile Jeremy's arm was well on the mend. The cast had been removed, and the dreadful scars had healed, but had left some swelling and lesions where the stitches had closed the wounds. He realized that it would never be as good as new but he also knew that he was very lucky to have the limb at all. He was told to exercise it gently and, perhaps, the stiffness would soon dissipate, but he would always experience some pain, probably for the rest of his life. Doctor Smith was well satisfied with the treatment he had received.

There was, however, the question of his army career. Commissions in the more elite regiments were much sought after, and had to be purchased, although would-be aspirants were first well vetted by the colonel, and Jeremy was no exception. Thus it was not a case of resigning, but whether he would be capable of military functions. The colonel of the 17th Lancers had decided to wait and see how capable Jeremy would be by the new year, some five months hence, and give him light duties so that he was able to be at home quite frequently.

And so, when the day came for Gerald and his orderly to come to Brush, Jeremy arranged to be there to help Fiona, and there was considerable excitement and a sense of anticipation of the arrival of the viscount. The closed carriage duly arrived and the first to alight was the orderly who introduced himself as Tom Oaks. He explained quietly that he did not wish to be disrespectful, but it would be appreciated if they would call him Tom, as that was how the patient knew him, and it was important to keep everything low key and not create any un-necessary changes.

He then helped Gerald down from the carriage. It had been emphasized that there should not be many people there to greet him as he easily became confused, so that only Alice and Fiona were present. The former had not seen her son recently as her visits to Chartham had become less frequent. But, physically, she saw little change although, perhaps, he had become stouter. He still wore a slight smile and his eyes were somewhat vacant. There was, obviously, little co-ordination between his brain and the rest of his body. Movements and actions had mostly become habit, and there seemed no sense of thought or of direction as one would expect of a normal mind. He was able to speak in a none-too clear voice, rather as a child who has just been taught the words. Of this they had been warned, nevertheless it was still something of a shock for Alice to see this grown man, mature in all else, but mindless. Who knows, thought Fiona, miracles can happen and perhaps one day the brain will 'click' back and memory will return. Stranger things have happened.

The summer days of that week came and went, and it was soon time for Tom Oaks to leave his patient. Together, with Fiona, they had succeeded in settling Gerald in his new and strange surroundings. It was soon obvious that he accepted Fiona and seemed to enjoy her company, so that Tom's departure was not as traumatic on the patient as they had feared. He said goodbye to Alice and Julian.

'It has been really nice meeting you, and I have to say that I am sorry to leave. Your son has settled far quicker than I expected, and I am happy to leave him in the capable hands of Miss Fortescue. She is a real professional and such a nice lady. I wouldn't be surprised to hear that your son's condition has improved because of her.'

Julian, in the weeks that followed, saw how happy his wife had become. She seemed to bloom, taking on a new lease of life now that her eldest son had returned home, and he enjoyed watching her fuss and busy herself helping to attend to Gerald's whims. Not that he was in any way demanding of attention, but appeared grateful for it nevertheless. The time would come when both she and Fiona would endeavour to help Gerald to speak with increasing intelligence for he was already showing signs of more understanding, and they were both becoming more and more confident of success.

Then one day Jeremy arrived, bursting with news. He had been spending most of his time in London at the headquarters of his regiment, coming home at odd intervals. 'Mother, tremendous news. You must come up to London next week. I am to receive a medal from the Queen herself, and you have been invited to the ceremony. It seems that several of the survivors of Balaclava and the other battles are to be rewarded. What do you think of that? Is it not marvellous?'

4

The first to recover from the announcement of this dramatic news, Julian was quick to congratulate his step-son.

'I am sure the whole country will applaud this recognition of your gallantry and of the others too. At least it goes some way to compensate for your dreadful ordeals, and Alice and I are very proud of you.' He paused for a moment. 'But this is your mother's moment. It must be her, and her alone, who should accompany you and witness your achievement, it should not be for me to intrude in your time of honour. Besides, my dear,' he turned to his wife, 'it is imperative for me to be in Sussex next week. The surveyors have hit a snag with one of the landowners who refuses to sell a parcel of land over which the new line is to run, and I really should meet him. I am sure you will understand, Jeremy.'

'Oh what a pity, Julian.' Alice was a little disappointed but, on the other hand, this would be her younger son's day of glory and it meant much to her to have him on her own and at the back of her mind she was relieved that her husband could not come.

Jeremy arranged for his mother to stay up in London that following week where he would entertain her and she could do some shopping. Fiona was quite capable of looking after the house, and anyway Julian would probably be back in a few days depending on his negotiations with the obstinate landowner.

The invention of the electric telegraph had brought untold benefits especially to the world of business, and in the last year the latest improvement had resulted in the automatic telegraph print-out, where instead of the morse code having to be translated into letters and words, they were now automatically printed out at the various receiving stations. As the telegraph wires were wont to follow the railway lines for ease of access and convenience, most of the by-stations had receiving machines with an operator, and Julian had been quick to have one installed at Brush Halt for his own use, together with the transmitter, so that he could both send and receive messages. With this in mind he arranged with Jeremy to inform him when he might expect Alice home, and could arrange transport. He was also able to send a message down the line to expect him at its head on the Monday.

Alice, accompanied by Jeremy, took the train to London where she was comfortably installed at Brown's Hotel, and later that evening enjoyed a show at the Gaiety Theatre. The investiture was to be held at St. James Palace on the Wednesday, so that the next day Alice was able to buy a suitable gown and thoroughly enjoy some shopping.

The great day arrived with sunshine and a cooling breeze. Arriving at the Palace, Jeremy encountered several friends who had survived the charge at Balaclava. There were men and officers from other regiments who were also to be decorated. The variety of uniforms made a dazzling array of colour, with splendidly adorned soldiers sporting shakoes, plumed helmets, and gold braid enhancing the multicoloured dress uniforms. Highly polished buttons and sword hilts sparkled in the sunlight, and they made a brave spectacle, rather different, Jeremy thought to himself, to the aftermath of the charge when the retreat showed only tattered uniforms covered in blood and gore.

Easy enough, on this bright summer's day in the heart of London crowded with sightseers and smartly dressed friends and relatives of those about to be honoured, to forget the desperate fighting in the Crimea, to forget those now in lonely graves in that outlandish spot. To forget the horrors of Scutari, the grievously wounded and the dying. The filth, the disease and the gangrenous limbs of the unfortunates, and the devoted care of Miss Nightingale and her fellow angels of mercy, to whom, including himself, so many were enabled to return home.

No, to forget should never be allowed, the memories should be kept alive if only to honour those who had fallen. Hopefully the sight of the decorated few would mean something to present and future generations. This gaily dressed company seen here, today, as the epitomy of English chivalry, might lift their spirits, but there was nothing gallant in the blood and mire of the battlefields!

Jeremy was jolted back to the present by a nudge from Alice. Names were being called out and lists consulted and ticked, and then they were ushered into an ante-room and segregated into groups, separated from their friends and relatives. Then the great doors of the audience chamber were thrown open, and as their names were called they advanced singly towards the throned monarch who was seated on a dais.

While waiting his turn Jeremy was able to look around and admire the setting of this great occasion. The Lord Chamberlain, the equerries, the lords and ladies-in-waiting. Among the throng he espied the arrogant face of Lord Cardigan himself amongst a clique of field marshalls and other high ranking officers. All this in stark contrast to the little figure of the Queen, who sat motionless upon her throne. A pale, rather podgy face showing little or no animation at the scene before her. She was dressed in a flowing dark blue gown gathered at her throat with the sash of the Order of the Garter her only embellishment. Upon her bare head sat a coronet of pearls. Slightly behind her stood Prince Albert whose look comprised both pride and adoration as he gazed at her. As the Prince Consort he was a popular figure to all and his wise and calm advice was well known.

The Queen had just completed dubbing the newest knight of the realm with her sword, and then the names were being called starting with the more important orders and decorations which were to be bestowed upon England's heroes. With a start Jeremy heard his name, and going forward to the dais he gave a deep bow. To his surprise he was favoured with a slight smile and with it a query as to the health of 'her old friend' Viscountess Emmerdale. The recipients of the investiture had been warned not to address Her Majesty unless asked directly a question, so he was able to say that his mother was in good health and was actually here with him.

'Please give her my good wishes and congratulate her on her brave son,' the queen said, and then proceeded to fasten the medal upon his chest.

'Thank you, ma'am, I will be happy to tell her.' He

81

bowed again and retreated.

Later that day, when he at last found himself alone with Alice after the round of parties and jollification which were inevitable on such an occasion, he was able to recount the queen's words and her greetings to 'her old friend'. Alice was delighted to be remembered and somewhat surprised.

'Oh, it was a long time ago, but fancy her remembering me. Actually it was your father and Prince Albert who were friendly. He was an equerry to the Prince in his younger days and in that capacity I was often at Court with him and invited to all sorts of public and private occasions. Of course, since your father died I left all that sort of thing behind me and have rarely thought about those grand days at Court.'

'Well I never.' Jeremy was astonished. 'You have never mentioned anything about that,a I had no idea you knew the queen.'

'Oh I would not say I knew her now. So much water has flowed under the bridge since our younger days, I hardly gave it a thought and am very honoured that Her Majesty should remember and have such nice things to say to you. Although, I have to admit that when I was in the palace I could not but think back to those halycon days when I was young and newly married, and life was full of fun, and to remember other similar occasions like today.'

'Poor mother, it must have been rather sad for you with such memories.'

'Oh I am not complaining. I did miss your father terribly for a while, and I fear that I did rather retire from public life. No, life is wonderful again, I have a wonderful caring husband. I would not have it any other way. And I have Gerald home again, and that

82

gives me a terrific incentive to help him. And I have you as well,' She squeezed her younger son's good arm. 'I've got you safe and sound and am very proud of you as I know your father would be too.'

They decided to stay a little longer in town revisiting old friends and going to the theatre again, and Jeremy, as agreed with Julian, despatched a telegraph message to advise of his mother's return on Friday. Jeremy had to stay in London but would hope to be back at Brush the following week, so the next day he saw her safely in to her reserved carriage in one of Julian's trains. She had thoroughly enjoyed herself these last few days, in which she had been present at her younger son's proud moment with the queen, witnessing the recognition of the bravery of so many fine colourfully uniformed soldiers, she had shopped, had been regaled at fine restaurants and entertained at the theatre, meeting many of her old friends. Now, she would be glad to return home and see how her other son was faring. She had few qualms on this issue having the fullest confidence in Fiona's caring attention and nursing expertise. Fiona had been given a bedroom adjoining Gerald so that she could be within hearing should anything occur at night, and so Alice had been quite content to leave Brush under these circumstances.

Within a few hours of his wife leaving in one direction, Julian was speeding towards Dover and the new terminus there. He had been informed that the new Bill in parliament gave him license to continue his railway right along the south coast taking in the various sea-ports and coastal towns *en route*. This was big business and his past success in rail transport had influenced financial backing to the extent that his confidence in the new line was limitless. However, his success to date was based on clear thinking countering his ambition to achieve his aims, so that he forebore reckless spending, and his bargaining for land franchise was careful.

To this end he needed to approach the recalcitrant landowner with caution. He would not bribe him by over-valuing the price of the land he sought, but by persuading him of the advantages that would ensue by having such a ready access to transport and perhaps offering a rail halt at the owner's choice of place. To this end he was successful, and he succeeded in his bargaining using the same technique as often before when opposition to the line's progress arose. He spent the rest of the day discussing the further route with his surveyors and general manager, then catching a train back he eventually arrived at Brush quite late that night.

Fiona heard the arrival of his carriage. She had retired to bed having seen to her patient's wants. She heard Julian ascending the stairs only to pause outside her door and then continue to his own apartment. Her heartbeat immediately quickened, and the now familiar physical call of her body began to make itself felt in her loins and her legs began to tingle. Apart from the servants away in the upper storey of the house and Gerald asleep next door, she was alone in the house with this man who stirred feelings in her which had until recently been completely dormant. In spite of herself she could not but let her imagination dwell on the consequences of this physical attraction. She knew that should Julian wish to possess her, which in her heart she realized that he did, she would be quite powerless to prevent it happening. She thought that Alice would be away for several nights and doubted her willpower to resist

Julian's total possession of her, although she must try if only to satisfy her conscience and retain her virginity. But did she really wish to remain a virgin? She knew by the reaction of her limbs to Julian's proximity, that passion was only waiting to be unleashed in no uncertain terms.

Eventually she fell into a dreamless sleep only to be suddenly awakened some hours later by an unearthly scream, although she did not realize what it was that had awoken her until it happened again. The sound came from next door, Gerald's room, and without even taking the time to put on a robe to cover her night attire, she scrambled out of bed and rushed to her patient's room. She found him sitting up in bed. He had had a nightmare, and later she was to realize that the very fact that he had been dreaming showed that his mind must be reawakening where previously it had seemed quite blank. When he saw her he seemed to relax almost immediately, and as she soothed him both by touch and words he was soon laying back on the pillows and peacefully asleep again.

Fiona turned and saw with a start that Julian was in the room, likewise with no robe, clad only in his nightshirt. Frantically she realized that only her thin nightdress concealed her nakedness, and buttoned to the neck and voluminous as it might be she felt wholly exposed to this man who was no more covered than she. She hastily averted her eyes, but not before she had glimpsed the hardening of his manhood, so different to that of those poor flaccid soldiers that she had nursed. Her feet remained rooted where she stood and she was unable to move.

Julian put his finger over his lips and nodded towards the now sleeping Gerald, willing her silence and then taking her hand in his he led her back to her room. She seemed to have lost any willpower to resist and followed him realizing what fate had now in store for her, her inherent shyness giving way to the subconscious desires of her body.

Back in her own room Julian closed the door and drew her towards him. Making a last tremendous effort to resist the inevitable outcome that she knew must surely happen, she at last found her voice.

'No Julian, please, I cannot, I must not, if only for your wife's sake, please leave me be.'

Her pleadings were stifled as his mouth found hers, moving gently on her lips, then with increasing pressure. At the same time his hand moved down to her buttocks, pressing her loins against his, and she gasped when she felt his male organ hard against her. In spite of herself her own body responded automatically, such was the power of their mutual attraction, and she knew now that nothing short of an earthquake would halt the eventual outcome of her seduction.

Reaching up to the buttons at her throat he slowly unfastened them still holding her tight against him. But when he went to slide the gown over her quivering shoulders, he found that the nightdress was not designed for this. Instead he had to use both hands to grasp the hem and draw it up her body and over her head. She made no further move to resist, allowing him to slowly reveal her naked body. As he had previously surmised, her slender legs gave way to slim thighs and hips to reveal a flat stomach, and then his eyes were riveted upon her small but perfectly proportioned jutting breasts. With a cry he threw aside her gown and holding her tightly about the waist lowered his head and almost devoured her nipples, such was his frantic desire for her.

Passion had now overtaken all thoughts of reluctance with Fiona, and this frenzied attack upon her breasts created an equal desire to discover what lay beneath Julian's covering, which she proceeded to remove, her exciting fingers groping for the fastenings and pulling the garment over his head, so that at last he stood in an equally naked state, and she gloried unashamedly in the sight of his throbbing manhood.

Julian picked up the totally unresisting girl and laid her on her bed with a cry of triumph, to gaze upon her perfection a final moment, before throwing himself upon her eagerly accepting body. It only needed two violent thrusts before he had penetrated her fully and she hardly felt the pain of her deflowering, so eager was she to receive him. His frantic motions soon were to be matched by her own and their orgasms were reached within seconds of each other.

Fiona felt no guilt when Julian finally relaxed his hold on her, but clung to him, caressing and kissing, unwilling to let him go. The guilt would come later when she understood the enormity of their actions, when she realized that Alice's husband had taken her as a mistress. Although she knew there was no future in it for her, she lay beside her lover eager to experience his passionate coupling once again.

For his part Julian rejoiced in his conquest of this woman, hardly daring to believe that she had finally been so receptive to his desires. She showed no distress in the fact that she had lost her virginity to him, a happily married man. He had wanted her from the moment he saw her in her new dress which had transformed her into a very desirable woman, quite the reverse of the hitherto nondescript female in her shoddy clothes.

His eyes again took in the naked beauty of this lovely girl who lay beside him, her lips parted and still moist from their kisses, and his arm that had loosely been holding her involuntarily tightened. As he drew her to him to touch again her flesh, desire again began to grip him. She was as eager to respond to his renewed caresses and as eagerly possessive as he again took her. This time he was able to prolong his lovemaking, and brought her to the peak of ardour again and again before releasing her so that she cried out in her extremity of passion. Julian was very fit and strong, so that he barely tired as he made love to her throughout the long night, but by early morning they were both exhausted, and so, reluctantly, he eventually returned to his own room.

The next day they both behaved decorously, although Fiona was full of shyness in his company, realizing what had occurred during the night, but unbelieving that she had been so capable of such unbridled lust, for that is what she accepted had happened. She would have been quite happy to have fallen in love with this fantastic man, but knew that this was not possible. She would not consider the possibility of Julian forsaking Alice for her, and so she supposed that she would have to be content with being his mistress, in secret she hoped. He had unlocked a passion she had not dreamt she possessed, and found it a joyous sensation which she could and would repeat whenever Julian wished. She was no hoyden. Julian was the only man to whom she would ever be able to give herself, and he was the only one she knew who would ever be able to provoke these feelings in her. She was quite fatalistic in that she knew that when Alice returned she must try and subdue these feelings, and behave as normally as she always did. It would be difficult but it had to be. So, she admitted, make hay while the sun shines! She almost hated her body for these unseemly desires, but oh, to be with her lover was wonderful.

So by night they made love and their passions were undiminished, rising again and again to the heights of ecstacy, and so mutual had it become that both were able to reach the point of release simultaneously, and for a while to lay in each other's arms without speaking, content to let their bodies take their temporary rest and communicate by touching.

The final night before Alice's return they tried to make special, both knowing that events must return to normality, and that Alice must not know of their involvement with each other. Fiona soon learned that there were many different ways to make love and was an eager pupil grateful for this worldly knowledge, and was enthusiastically responsive, happily returning Julian's passionate tutelage that she would remember and always treasure.

With Alice's return life for both of them returned to normal, with Fiona happily continuing her care of Gerald, but in her heart she rejoiced that her femininity had fulfilled its bodily function, and achieved a purpose that hitherto she had been unaware. There were moments when in Alice's company Fiona felt a sense of guilt that she had betrayed her, but that was only momentary and easily forgotten when she relived the ecstacies that her union with Julian had brought about. If it were never again to be repeated she had at least the memories, but somewhat wickedly was prepared to allow Julian access to her bed should the opportunity arise.

Without realizing the whys and wherefores it was as if she had tasted some drug, which having released unknown sensations, she would crave for again and again.

Summer was drawing in, halcyon days for all of them. The railway was progressing very favourably and Julian had received several offers of investment from those who saw the future of a south coast railway line. However, he was restless in seeking ways and means for using his energy in all directions. More improvements to the house and the estate he discussed with Alice who let him have his way with smiling encouragement.

One day he returned from a business trip where he had by chance met a certain Mr Doulton. The flushed water closet had recently been put on the market, and one of the first to install the system had been the queen. Up to now the sewage system of many great houses had been primitive and unhygienic to say the least, and the outside 'privy' was still the usual method. Although many had started to install water systems, the automatic flushing lavatories were in their infancy. Julian's inventive mind allied to his engineering knowledge set to work to improve a method that he determined to install at Brush Hall, and his encounter with Mr Doulton had given him new ideas.

There was a sewage system of sorts at the Hall, with a drain pipe running to an enclosed pit which had to be emptied frequently with the resulting miasma of disagreeable smells. The closets had to be flushed by hand along a vertical pipe, and here hygiene was very much in its infancy. It was only recently that the connection between disease and the lack of hygiene was being realized, and disinfectants were scarce.

Cholera, typhus and typhoid were still rife in the poorer sections of the towns, where the crowded state of the houses encouraged vermin and the fleas they carried, spreading the germs of disease.

Julian was in his element designing new plans and ideas and would be seen in the company of a well known engineer or a builder surveying a layout of drains, or discussing the natural fall of land. Before work could be started it was necessary to find a manufacturer who could construct the vital parts of the system. Autumn was upon them before they realized it and so it was decided to carry out the work the following spring.

Fiona's passionate liaison had only been repeated once since the week when Alice was away, and that had been rather unsatisfactory and hurried. Nevertheless Fiona was content knowing that Julian's desire for her remained unabated. Then, early one morning some weeks later, she awoke feeling sick and unwell. She had missed one menstrual period, but put it down to her sexual activity upsetting the normal course of events, but now it was two months late, and with awful certainty she guessed that she was probably pregnant. Neither had considered the possible aftermath of their fervent coupling, but ruefully she understood that Julian might well have impregnated her.

Eventually, having vomited several times, she dressed and came downstairs feeling ghastly and looking pale and ill. It was impossible to hide the symptoms from Alice, who was full of concern for her and soon packed her off to bed. She suggested sending for the doctor but Fiona managed to dissuade her saying that she would be all right the next day. In fact she did feel better later on, but the following morning was sick again.

That day Alice came to her room in some anxiety. Holding the girl's hand, she said, 'You are pregnant, aren't you, my dear? How long is it since you had your last period?'

Fiona was aghast that her secret fear should be so quickly discerned and burst into tears.

'There now, my dear, it is not the end of the world, but you may well find it difficult to account for your condition.' Alice paused a moment as Fiona continued to weep. 'It was my husband, wasn't it?'

'How did you know?' Fiona whimpered. 'Oh what will become of me?'

Alice smiled grimly. 'Oh I could see that he was attracted to you from the time you wore that new dress. I cannot really blame him for that. You are a very attractive young woman and he is very hot blooded, and I doubt that at my age I can satisfy him for long. I do not suppose that you are the first. Many women of my age have learned to accept their husband's occasional infidelity as long as it remains discreet. But I am afraid that you will have to leave here much as I regret losing you. You must go back to Miss Sellon. I will write to her and explain the situation.'

Fiona nodded miserably. She had not really come to terms with the eventual outcome of her attraction for Julian. She had been ecstatically happy at Brush these last months, and had given little thought to the future. Now she had to realize that there would be no future with Julian, and the affair had to end. Alice read her thoughts.

'It is not the end of the world,' she repeated. 'You will have the baby and your memories of how it came to be conceived. I will see that you are properly looked after and that Julian makes some financial arrangement for your upkeep and that of the child. After all,' she added severely, 'it has to be his responsibility, but only if it is kept quite secret. I want no scandal at Brush, young lady.'

Later Alice confronted her husband telling him of Fiona's condition. Julian was devastated. He too had given little thought to the possible outcome of his torrid encounters with Fiona. If he had considered it at all it was with the subconscious hope that there would be no resulting pregnancy. He was still in love with Alice, but as she so rightly surmised she was unable to satisfy his sexual needs, and the close proximity of the girl had stirred an overwhelming desire.

'I know that you can never forgive me, my dear, I can make no excuses, but should you be able to come to terms with what I have done to you I will try and control myself, and hope to continue to be your loving husband.'

'Oh yes, but it is just as much my fault, I suppose. Unwittingly putting temptation in your path. Men, I suppose, must be men. Fiona will go back to Miss Sellon, and I will see that the girl is properly looked after, and I have told her that you will be responsible for her financially in the future. You will see your lawyer and make all the arrangements in the next day or so.'

5

Alice had been worried that, with the departure of Fiona, Gerald's condition would deteriorate as these last weeks he had seemed to increasingly depend on the girl who looked after him with such devotion. Rather than hire another nurse to take the girl's place, thus presenting her son with a stranger, she decided to nurse him herself. Having seen almost as much of his mother as of Fiona latterly, she was gratified that there was no relapse to his previous rather torpid state. In fact the opposite was the case. It seemed that he was beginning to think more for himself, and was adjusting his mind more and more to what was happening around him. She did not dare hope that his memory would ever return in full, but he seemed no longer like a helpless child, and had begun to do more and more for himself.

If Julian missed Fiona he showed no sign except to devote himself to his wife, and throw himself with increased energy into his work on the railway. He still found enough time to continue to put into practice ideas and schemes to enhance the house, including arranging for a gang of labourers to dig out the new drains and cess-pit. He had negotiated a financial settlement for his former mistress, and a trust would be set up for the child later on. Alice had written to

Miss Sellon but had not gone into detail. Whether that redoubtable lady had suspected any connivance on Alice's part she kept her silence and made no further query as to the reason of Fiona's return to London, except to say that she would take good care of her.

Alice began to enjoy having Gerald to herself, and, probably, in her innermost thoughts was content to look after him without the help of Fiona. Life for her was good and the village people began to see much more of her than they had for some years. She enjoyed taking her son for drives in the countryside, but preferred her old governess cart, which had been fully restored, pulled by Dobbin, to the swanky cabriolet that Julian had bought. It seemed to do Gerald good and he came to look forward to their forays and after several trips seemed to be able to recognize people they stopped to chat with. She had great hopes that, perhaps in the not too distant future, a partial recovery might happen. Certainly he was no trouble and was amenable to whatever arrangements his mother made for him. The main problem was, of course, his speaking ability and the whole household made a special effort to help in this at every opportunity. Later, Alice decided, she would employ a tutor to coach him in what one day would be known as speech therapy.

She had accepted Julian's infidelity knowing that she would never be able to satisfy his virility herself, and, as in so many other households of her class, this was a sign of the times. So long as discretion was absolute, women found that if having a mistress kept their husbands compliant and satisfied, they would accept the situation as the lesser evil. Although they still shared the same bed Julian seldom made sexual overtures, and on the rare occasions when he did so Alice accepted him but without the fervour that they had previously enjoyed. No doubt, eventually, her husband would find another mistress with whom he would be able to consummate his passion, but it would be a long time before he would do so at Brush Hall. She admitted to herself that they were good friends and life together was reasonably tolerable.

It was November and the advent of winter began to chill the evening air. The leaves on the trees in all their russet glory began to fall, and soon the lawns and driveway lay under a scattering of dying foliage to be raked up, only to be covered again within a day or so. Alice always regretted the passing of summer, and hitherto had dreaded the onset of winter. Previously, before she met Julian, she had been content to retire indoors at the first sign of winter frosts and fog to the warmth of the big house, hence becoming even more of a recluse.

This year however she was to be seen busily instructing the gardeners in their work. She was planning new herbaceous borders and, on Julian's suggestion, the renovation of the walled kitchen garden which had become neglected and forlorn, with an infestation of weeds and rubbish. The crumbling brick walls were repaired and new paths with box edging created and it was gradually restored to its former splendour. She would stand and gaze towards the old house, now resplendent with new paint, and marvel that so much had been achieved in so short a time due to Julian's untiring enthusiasm to restore and enhance their home. It really had become a home, not somewhere she lived if, she grimaced, it could have been called living, where for so many years she had shut herself away, and life had just drifted by. She smiled to herself when she remembered the day when she had taken one of her increasingly infrequent forays into the country in the governess cart, and Julian's engine had so frightened poor Dobbin. Such is fate. She wondered what else fate might have in store for her. She subconsciously castigated herself for such thoughts. It would do no good trying to conjure up the future. Life was good today. To be content with the present was important, to enjoy the life that was left to her.

There was, however, another side to the coin. The last few days had seen Julian making more than his usual trips to London, and after each journey it seemed that some problem was worrying him, for he became morose and was sleeping badly. After a week of this Alice, who hitherto had been averse to discuss his business, tackled him, asking him if she could help.

'Is it that obvious, my dear? I am sorry. I had been hoping to settle this business without bothering you, but I would value your good sound common sense.'

On receiving a reassuring nod he continued. 'It seems that the South Western Railway are becoming alarmed by the speed and extent of my new line from Dover. You understand that, although their line has been in existence for a year or so, it goes direct to the west and does not take in the south coast towns along the way. Now they have suddenly woken up to the fact that my new line is going to take much of their trade, both in passenger traffic and the transit of heavy goods.'

'I can guess what's coming next,' Alice interrupted. 'They want to stop your line before it comes into competition with theirs.'

'That's about it, although it is somewhat more

devious. You are, of course, aware that I have several backers who have put money into my company. I would not have been able to have achieved my successes with only my own capital, and so I issued shares according to the capital invested, which in fact is really a glorified loan, but without which I could not have proceeded.'

He paused a moment to collect his thoughts. 'The other day I was talking to one of them when he told me that he had been approached by my rivals with an offer to buy his shares at a price vastly in excess of their present value. He, apparently, deferred any decision but contacted one or two of the other investors who told the same story. And so, if these gentlemen do decide to sell, it will put me out on a limb, and no doubt they will then decide to take over my company with the majority of the shareholders leaving me with less than the capital with which I started.'

'But can they just do that? It sound immoral to me. After all the hard work you have put into the business, apart from the expertise and initiative you provided.'

'Oh yes, it is what they call "taking over" a company by acquiring a majority shareholding, quite legal, but hardly ethical and rather frowned upon by the banking houses. But I have no doubt this method is here to stay, and in years to come it may become standard practice. Let someone clever enough start a new idea and then, when it is established, force them to sell by bribing the investors.'

'But that's unfair. You have been clever enough to beat them and now they want to rob you. What are you going to do? I don't suppose that I can help much, but I do know a few important people who still wield some influence in the government if that might help.'

He stooped to kiss her fondly. 'We might have to come back to that, but I have some ideas that we must explore first. I have been up to town several times lately, as you know, and have been concocting a scheme with one of my backers. He has been making some enquiries of his own, and it seems that the South Western, far from being profitable, are running at a loss, and know that our own line is going to be a winner given time, and that is what we need. You see it will be a year or two before my line will be fully operational, before it starts to earn any money let alone a profit. And so Lord Flannery is to meet my other shareholders and persuade them, hopefully, to hang on and not to sell. Who knows, there might come a time, not so far off, that my railway will be in a position to buy my rival or even to sell at a figure which will enable me to retire a rich man!'

'You will never retire and forget rail pioneering. I would be willing to wager that you would start something similar in another area. You are not the type to retire gracefully, your mind is far too active.' And so is your body, she thought to herself. Far too virile for your age. 'Besides which,' she went on aloud, 'what would I do with you hanging about the place all day? I suppose you would dream up some other scheme. After the new drains – what next?'

'Funny you should say that, my dear, there was another idea I was thinking about . . .'

Alice threw up her hands in mock despair.

'I knew it! No, don't tell me, I cannot bear it.'

Julian laughed and placed his arm about her shoulders.

'You might just approve of this. It was a thought

that came to me the other day. Your Jeremy will be marrying one day, and it is possible he might wish to live nearby when he retires from the army, and I don't suppose his wife would want us, two old fogies, in the way. She will want her own home to rear your grandchildren I am sure.'

Alice held her breath not sure what was coming next as he continued, 'So I was considering along the lines of building a house for them at the top end of the park, far enough away from the Hall but not so far so you can see them at any time. What do they call it?'

'Oh yes, a dower house, that is what it would be. But can we really afford it? I would not know the cost of building, but why should you spend your hard earned money on my family?'

'It is my family, too,' Julian replied quietly. 'I want to do as much as I can for us. Apart from that we can call it an investment, an enhancement if you like, to the estate, and it can still belong to us, if you would prefer that. That is another reason why it is so desperately important to stave off any encroachment from our rivals in their attempts to impoverish me through taking over my railway.'

The next week was an anxious time for both of them as negotiations in London proceeded. It soon appeared that Lord Flannery had persuaded his fellow bankers to stay with Julian and resist the rival offer, but the third investor, who was a well known industralist, had not made up his mind. His attitude harboured on the adage that 'a bird in the hand was worth two in the bush', and that, he explained to Lord Flannery, was how he liked to invest his money – to bet on a sure thing! It was realized that without his support they could still continue their railway, but an unanimous front would prove far more successful in dissuading the South Western Company from pursuing their scheme for any future incursions against Julian.

He now decided to take te bull by the horns and proceed with the building of the 'Dower House'. And so, one sunny November afternoon, wrapped up against the chill air, he and Alice walked across the park to the spot Julian had in mind. The lane ran round that end of the parkland, the same lane where Julian first met Alice. They walked by the new avenues of beech trees that had been planted earlier that year, and Alice examined them to see whether any had died. Some still had a few leaves which were now brown and shrivelled, but all showed signs of healthy growth.

The park was dotted with mature oaks and beeches which in summer gave a welcoming shade for the cattle grazed there by a local farmer, and Alice spoke about how she first came here as a young bride to the home of her first husband whose family had lived at Brush Hall for generations, and then of the lonely days when he had been away fighting Napoleon's armies.

The site that Julian had in mind was in a curved corner of the park debouching onto the lane, which was secluded by a couple of giant oaks which must have been planted many years before the Hall was built. Looking back across the gently sloping sward Alice could glimpse the rooftop of her home which nestled in the slight hollow, and she agreed with her husband's estimate that the proposed dower house would be just the right distance away. She was becoming as enthusiastic as he and was already planning in her mind the sort of design and size of the project.

'I am none too keen on the present-day idea of architecture with all its frills, turrets and what-nots. Far too fussy and impractical. What do you think, dear?'

'Rather as you; I think something on a smaller scale to the Hall. Simple but dignified, practical and space saving. We could get the architect to give us a few ideas. Large windows, perhaps, but easy to keep warm on winter days, that is important.'

They were silent for some moments, both engrossed in thought.

'We must talk to Jeremy,' said Alice. 'I wonder whether he has a lady friend, he never mentions any female involvement – we shall have to encourage him! It really would be wonderful to see grandchildren running around.' She gazed fondly at her husband. 'And now I am getting broody.'

As it happened Jeremy came home that weekend, and after dinner was gently quizzed by his mother as to what thoughts, if any, he had given to his future in the army.

'I have not given it serious thought. There was a time when the army meant everything to me, and they have been good to me since the war. On the other hand I can never be a fighting soldier again with this arm, so it means administrative employment at which I am none too good. I think that what I would really like is a training job in the cavalry, you know, teaching the art of fighting from the saddle.'

'Of course, my darling, but you will have to think about settling down soon before you are that much older, and perhaps your arm may well be a blessing in disguise. With your knowledge of horses you have to be an asset to the cavalry and you could be at home more often.'

He smiled. 'You know, if I did not know you better, I would say that you were up to something!'

Their answering looks betrayed them. 'Ha, you are up to something, what are you planning? Come on, out with it.'

Julian answered as Alice blushed. 'Your mother has been hoping that sooner rather than later there might be a lady involved. I think she might like to see some grandchildren about the place. Not my business, of course,' he coughed, 'but the same goes for me too, a sort of surrogate grandfather, yes, I'd like that too.' He continued quickly, forestalling Jeremy's interjection. 'Then there is something else that we should like to do. This would involve you one day, soon we hope. We think that the estate needs what we have called a dower house. Another home, a modern building at the far end of the park. There is a slight rise in the land, and it would be well sited and will enhance the Hall and add to its value.' Julian continued to expand on that theme and his audience gave him his head knowing how he enjoyed riding a new 'hobby-horse'.

'Well I never,' Jeremy found his voice. 'You never cease to astonish me, and what a wonderful idea, building a house I mean. Even if there was no lady involved it would still be most acceptable.' He smiled. 'As a matter of fact there might well be someone, although I have not as yet popped the question. But with this very generous suggestion for a home there could be a happy affirmative before very long.'

Alice put both her arms around her son and hugged him. 'Now that's something every mother likes to hear. Knowing my son I expect she will be a wonderful girl and you will make each other very

103

happy. Hurry up and ask her and bring her here to see us just as soon as you can. Meanwhile I will get an architect to draw up some plans and give us some ideas.'

They continued to discuss the sort, size and kind of house they had in mind.

'The timing should be just right, by the time that we have agreed on the details, arranged the survey and the builders, it will be early spring and work can be started; and perhaps we shall have the occupants ready to move in!' Julian grinned. 'Incidentally that will fit in very nicely with the new drainage system, and the new house can be included.'

Alice explained how Julian was dissatisfied with the present facilities at the Hall.

'I suppose I have grown used to its inadequacies after all these years never having known anything different. It is not really the sort of subject I would normally discuss, I mean drains are a necessity but something in the background, and definitely not drawing-room talk! But Julian says they are in a very unhealthy state and anyway this Mr Doulton has invented something far superior.'

'Yes, we have heard all about that in London, and there is no doubt that his ideas are definitely in vogue now that the queen is installing the system. I have to congratulate you on your initiative, but won't it be terribly expensive? I don't want to seem rude and I am very conscious of your generosity, and really do appreciate it.'

'I like to consider it an investment if you insist, said Julian. 'Your mother has given me a real home and a ready made family and this is my way of sharing things. As long as the future smiles on us let us make the most of it.'

Next morning the weather still held good, so they walked across the park with Gerald to show Jeremy the site that Julian had chosen.

'Gerald and I used to play up here when we were kids. There was a special partly hollow oak tree which we called our house. Yes, there it is, still standing and looking just the same. Come on, Gerald, see if you remember it.'

Jeremy led his brother to the old tree, and together they walked around it, and then Jeremy ducked inside the half-hollow trunk. To the amazement of the others, who had followed, Gerald was trying to say something. His speech was inarticulate, but the words 'our tree' were decipherable and he was smiling broadly as he tried to join his brother and to clasp his arm. Jeremy continued to talk, willing his brother to answer and to remember their childhood games. Gradually, haltingly, further words could be discerned as he struggled to make himself understood. It was obvious that he knew what he wanted to say, but the frustrated effort of concentration brought beads of sweat to his forehead. With a little cry of happiness Alice rushed over and hugged her eldest son, and then they were all grinning. Gerald was now beaming with a broad smile and returned his mother's embrace.

'The mind is extraordinarily complex,' Julian remarked a little later. 'It takes some little incident like that to trigger off a memory that has been hidden in the subconscious, and then it seems to come together. I think that now Gerald has found out that he can convey his thoughts, however inarticulately, the will to speak will grow. But we must not let him become frustrated; let nature take its course. We must not rush it.'

It was Jeremy who made the suggestion that evening at dinner. Although he included all of them, it was Julian to whom he spoke.

'Christmas is nearly here, do you think it might be a good idea if we had a special celebration, a sort of climax to a rather special year?'

'Of course we should make a special seasonal occasion, had you something particular in mind? Your mother and I hardly had the chance last year, and we were just beginning a new life, but Christmas is always a family time, and we should celebrate as you rightly say.'

'Actually I was thinking of something more ambitious. You have made this house into such a lovely place it is about time you showed it off a bit. In fact I had in mind a party, perhaps even a dance. We could invite several friends of yours and mine from London, and also perhaps locally. We would not be able to put them all up for the night but I expect something could be arranged. It was just an idea but the more I think about it the better it seems. A Christmas Eve dance with all the festive trimmings would be marvellous.'

Alice clapped her hands. 'That is a good idea, what do you think Julian?'

'I thought that I was the one to have new ideas, but I have to admit I had not thought of that. It is an excellent thought, Jeremy, and we will really do it well. It shall be a Christmas that we will always remember and make it memorable for our guests. Now that you have suggested it allow me to add the trimmings.' He considered for a moment. 'We will have a marquée on the lawn. We will import caterers . . .' his mind ran on with ideas and suggestions, 'and how about a special train? We could run one from

106

London at a convenient time for our friends and perhaps a specially late one for their return. That could save trouble and the need to stay the night, if they are agreeable.'

They each had ideas and so their plans expanded from the nucleus of Jeremy's original suggestion. The discussion continued well into the evening, and they eventually retired to their beds happily satisfied with such an eventful day. Although Alice had been excited with Jeremy's Christmas Eve ideas, it was the seemingly miraculous return of her eldest son's memory that affected her most. Long after her husband's gentle love-making she lay awake thinking of how it had come about, whilst Julian breathed quietly asleep beside her. It seemed that a childhood incident had triggered Gerald's memory. Perhaps it was the combination of several half-forgotten juvenile memories which had jolted his brain cells out of their dormant state. But the whys and wherefores were irrelevant to Alice. If Gerald was to recover, her cup would indeed be full to overflowing with the happiness she had for so long ceased to expect. It was almost too good to be true; would that nothing should occur to ruin this new life.

December was with them and there was little time to make all the necessary arrangements. A list of guests was considered, both locally, and from London. Julian was to contact contractors for the installing of a marquée and the accessories, including a specially laid floor for the dancing. A small orchestra was to be engaged and Alice set about the catering requirements. Jeremy went back to London to contact the fellow officers who were to be invited, and help make arrangements from there.

Alice was in her element. Nothing so exciting as this

had happened for such a long time and it brought back the heady days when her first husband was alive and so much time was spent at Court attending dances and parties. All had ceased with the viscount's long illness after Waterloo, leading to her final retirement from the life that she had enjoyed so much. And now, a new husband, and a new life was beginning which she should not have the right to expect at her age. She thought that very few women were as fortunate as she, and come what may she would always have had this year to cherish and remember.

6

A long way away, many miles east of the Kent
countryside, the war in the Crimea was drawing to a
close. Sebastopol, so long beseiged by the allied forces
of England and France, finally succumbed, and the
Russians sought an armistice. The seige had lasted
many bitter months, and the previous winter had
seen the bitterest weather ever experienced by the
allied soldiers. The commissariat of the British had
suffered from administrative confusion, laziness and
timidity. Added to which the callousness and
stupidity of the staff had resulted in shortages of
food, clothing, shelter and animal fodder. Then the
catastrophe of that winter had resulted in a complete
breakdown in the distribution of what little was
available.

The previous year had seen the disastrous charge
of the Light Brigade at Balaclava, the decimation of
the cream of British cavalry. Many had managed to
reach the allied lines grievously wounded, and a few
were more fortunate in being only lightly scarred.
One of the luckier ones was Corporal Wilson, Jeremy
Lindley's orderly, who had ridden by the latter's side
during the advance, only to lose sight of him in the
retreat. The last sighting had been when Jeremy was
hit in the arm and had taken off at a furious gallop,

reins gripped in his teeth. Wilson had to take a different route when a party of Russian Cossacks had blocked his path.

When he eventually reached safety, Corporal Wilson began to look for his officer, but such was the confusion of the wounded men and horses, that darkness finally put an end to his search. All he could learn was that the more seriously wounded had been taken to the field hospital where amputations and operations were taking place. Later he was to find out that most of the survivors needing hospital treatment were being shipped over the water to Scutari on the mainland.

Having seen to his exhausted horse in the regimental stables where he found but a scattering of the survivors' mounts, all equally exhausted from the recent battle, he finally made his way back to his quarters. There he met up with others of his troop who had escaped the carnage, some bandaged, some miraculously unharmed, all with a lack-lustre demeanour, sitting about and suffering from shock. Heads raised as he came in and wan smiles greeted him. Later they were to recount their individual experiences, but for the moment they were content to rest and soon to sleep, mentally and physically exhausted.

The next day they were left to their own devices, ministering to their horses, some of which needed veterinary attention, and it was not until another day had passed that they were mustered along with the survivors of other regiments. It was to be in another theatre of the war that a mixture of those left from other regiments were to be sent. The seige of Sebastopol marked the beginning of the end of the war, but apart from skirmishes with groups of

Russian Cossacks who attempted to disrupt the allied encircling forces, there was little to do.

Winter weather soon put an end to further fighting. It was so bitter, and the clothing so completely inadequate, that Corporal Wilson spent those freezing weeks huddled around a brazier sharing a bivouac with his companions. However the horses had to be exercised daily in spite of the treacherous conditions underfoot. Disease amongst the troops was still rife, with dysentery, cholera and some typhoid cases reported daily. Far more soldiers died from the cold and disease than from the Russian sword.

Gradually the weather improved and grew warmer, resulting in increased activity and further assaults on the town. The cavalry were now able to make forays further afield, and it was not long before the Cossack threat was eliminated. With the summer the Russians had had enough, and called for a truce. The allies became masters of Sebastopol.

The long war was over and the victors took stock of the situation. Supplies of food and animal fodder were barely adequate, and the relieved town was starving. In order to alleviate these shortages, the obvious priority was to evacuate as many of the troops as possible and send them home. Even more important, however, was the evacuation of the sick and walking wounded, including those still in the hospitals. The task was enormous. There were some ships available and these were made ready immediately. The hospital ships were to include staff to help care for the sick and wounded. Corporal Wilson found himself with others of his regiment drafted for this purpose, as their horses were to travel on another vessel. They were none too happy with this, for apart from the prospect of an onerous job and doubtless an unpleasant one, they had so far managed to avoid the contagious diseases that had raged amongst the allies, the worst being cholera, from which many had died in most distressing ways. Generally aggravated by the lack of hygiene it was ferociously contagious amongst those living closely together.

There ensued a hive of activity. Clearing up the camp sites, hauling equipment and guns to the quayside, and transporting the sick. By the time the first ships were ready to sail summer was over and October was well on the way. Corporal Wilson and his mates had made themselves as comfortable as only a soldier knows how, and they were looking forward to being back in England, although what destiny had in store for them no one knew. Many, no doubt, would be demobilized as the army returned to a peace-time level, although there were rumours of troubles in the Far East. The British Empire was so far flung, and distances so vast, that it had proved more satisfactory to maintain complete military strength in each country, generally recruited as native troops with British officers and staff, as in the case of India.

But it was not until November that Corporal Wilson and his colleagues eventually left the Crimea, and commenced the slow voyage home. Within a day or two their troubles began. One or two cases, at first, and then more were diagnosed as cholera. The surgeons at the hospital had considered the patients to be clear of the disease, but obviously one or more had already contracted it before embarkation, and in the close confines of the ship the virus could spread rapidly.

Great efforts were made to segregate further suspected cases but the task was well nigh impossible. It was inevitable that Wilson and the others were involved, and another day saw the first death and the hasty burial at sea. As one day followed another further deaths occurred and it soon became obvious that there was little the doctors and staff could do to prevent even the healthy becoming infected.

Corporal Wilson was spending as much time on deck as possible hoping that the salt sea air would prove an antidote, but unfortunately for him, as the contagion spread, he became more and more involved with the sick and dying, and although he took every precaution, as did his friends, he feared that he too might succumb. Various methods were tried such as dipping kerchiefs in salt water and tying them over nose and mouth, and washing in salt water. Such rudimentary hygiene might well have helped stay the spread of the disease if the whole ship and its crew could have done likewise, but the germs were voracious in discovering the weaknesses and spreading into hitherto healthy bodies.

One morning some days later, when the ship had cleared the great Rock of Gibraltar, Corporal Wilson had a violent bout of diarrhoea which left him weak and exhausted. Although he had dreaded catching the cholera he did not immediately associate the symptoms as such, as there was no following pain. He put it down to something he had eaten the previous evening, as the ship's food was far from fresh and notorious in causing stomach cramps. But an hour or so later he was violently sick, eventually vomiting only liquid bile. He developed an unquenchable thirst which left him restless and exhausted.

He knew then that the worst had happened. He collapsed on his bunk and warned his colleagues to keep away from him lest they too succumbed. All day and all night he lay there, sometimes with fever other times shivering and vomiting bile, waiting for the inevitable claim of another victim. A second day passed as he lay alone, semi-conscious and past caring, his mind delirious.

On the third day the fever eased and his mind began to clear. He was no longer sick but a tremendous lassitude affected his limbs. Some time later, when he woke from a dreamless sleep, his mind was quite clear, and he no longer ached and began to feel hungry. With a tremendous effort he forced his legs to the deck grimacing at the dreadful mess of vomit. Holding on to any support he could grasp, he fought a spell of dizziness that threatened to collapse him back to the bunk, and staggered from his quarters.

Eventually he managed to reach the deck and was partially revived by the fresh salt breeze. Several of his friends saw him and stared amazed, having given him up for dead. Seeing them he managed to croak a request for food and a crock of water whilst holding on to the ship's rail to prevent him falling.

He gradually regained his strength over the remainder of the journey home, being looked after by his friends, until finally the white cliffs of Dover came into sight.

As they approached Ramsgate's outer harbour they could see a whole convoy of ambulances and other horse-drawn vehicles with a large welcoming crowd. The last thing that Wilson wanted was to be carted off to hospital as a convalescent, so he persuaded his comrades to mention nothing about his illness. So it was that when the last of the sick had been disembarked, Wilson and the others marched on to the quay to be formed up and the roll called. Finally they were taken to the regimental barracks to be re-kitted, and on the following day were sent home on leave.

Corporal Wilson was at some pains to discover what fate had befallen Captain Lindley, and requested an interview with the adjutant, who knew all about Jeremy's part in the epic battle. He was able to assure Wilson that Jeremy recovered from his wounds, and was probably at his home, although he was still attached to the Lancers. Being his erstwhile orderly the adjutant was prepared to authorize extra leave for Wilson so that he could visit his captain if he wished and gave him a travel warrant for that purpose.

'Did you know, Corporal, that he was decorated by the queen? Well deservedly too. But of course you were with him at the time, weren't you? Have you made any report yet on the action? Because I think you should; although you seem to have come through the fight unscathed, I should imagine you and others would be eligible for decoration.'

'Thank you sir. No, no one has mentioned anything about that. How would I go about it?'

The other thought for a moment. 'I will have a word with the colonel. Can you give me a list of your group now, and you all come back here tomorrow morning, say at ten o'clock, and we can go through it together. To tell you the truth, corporal, we have had very few actual accounts from individuals and I expect there will be further survivors from Balaclava who deserve recognition, though that's not for me to say.'

Corporal Wilson rejoined his friends and re-counted what the adjutant had told him.

'So you see we had better get our stories right, and tell 'em that happened to us and how we got back, whatever we can remember.'

They nodded, then one of them voiced the thoughts of many of them.

'I can't spell proper, so I can't write nothing.'

'Nor me, either,' echoed several of the others. One or two could write, but they all agreed that it would have to be done properly.

'Tell you what,' Wilson said after thinking about the problem. 'You all get your stories straight and we'll go together to the officer tomorrow, and get him to write it down for us. I should have thought of that before when I was talking to him; all right?'

They nodded and decided to try and remember all that had happened that dreadful day, and retired to their quarters to gather their thoughts.

The next day they all went to find the adjutant and explain the situation. He understood fully.

'I haven't the time just now but I'll get my clerk to do it for you in the correct manner and on some official paper.' He got up and went to find his clerk. They were taken to another room where their stories were written down. After an hour or so busily writing and asking questions the clerk was finished, and the numerous sheets of paper were collected and taken back to the adjutant after each trooper had put his name or mark on his respective account. He glanced through several and, shaking his head, said, 'Well I never. Some of these stories are quite extraordinary. I realize now that I never had any idea of what you chaps went through. You must have had a terrible time, and for what?' To himself he wondered who on the staff in the Crimea had been responsible for such an incredible blunder.

It was now December, and Wilson decided that he had better go and see his mother and father and spend Christmas with them. His home was not far away in neighbouring Sussex, and after Christmas he would go and find Captain Lindley. The thought occurred to him that, perhaps, the latter could find him a job. He had had enough of the army, and had no wish to go to war again in some far off country. Perhaps a job with horses. He was good with animals, he understood them and they him.

His mind made up he made his way home. It would be a good home-coming. He knew that his parents had been anxious about him, but they had no idea that he was back in England. He would surprise them. He was feeling almost fit again, something he had not expected after being so ill a week or so ago. He wondered what had been the cause, it surely could not have been cholera. Very few ever recovered from that dreaded disease, none that he had ever heard about anyway. But he had been in contact with those that had died aboard ship, and in spite of all the precautions that he had taken, he could quite easily have contracted the virus himself. But he was all right now.

His parents were overjoyed to see him. They had heard from the War Office that he had survived the fighting and that he would be repatriated in due course, but had no idea that he had returned.

They thoroughly spoiled him. Appalled at his thinness, his mother fed him all his favourite food, spending most of her time in the kitchen the next day.

He recounted over and over the charge of his brigade at Balaclava. Of the different acts of bravery he had either seen for himself or had heard from others. Of Captain Lindley galloping away holding the reins of his horse in his teeth and resting his shattered arm on the pommel of his saddle. How he had seen him break his sabre on a Russian's helmet. Some of the more gory stories might have sickened

117

some, but his father was an old soldier and both knew all about the horrors of battle, the maiming and killing, the thunder of guns with the rattle of musketry; the gallantry and the pageant of the many coloured uniforms. His father had seen it all before but did not tire from hearing it again.

He enjoyed a quiet Christmas with his parents only interrupted by the many well-wishers who had learned that he had just returned from the war, and anxious to hear more about the gallant charge of the six hundred. This he was glad to relate to them, sometimes embellishing his story with some exaggeration here and there, regaling his listeners with the dramatic events. They listened to him with wonder, and something akin to awe.

Having told his father and mother what he had learned of the fate of his gallant captain, they agreed that it would be right and proper that he should try and see him. If Captain Lindley was indeed at his home at Brush this should not be too difficult, because they had heard that there was now a railway line that passed by there.

Wilson stayed at home over Boxing Day and the next day he left, arriving in London having been given lifts on various conveyances, the owners of which were only too glad to listen to his stories. In his new uniform of a trooper of the 17th Lancers, he was quite eye-catching with the sky-blue tunic and gold trimmings, and the crimson shako upon his head. He therefore found no trouble in receiving offers of transport. In London he learned that there were indeed trains running regularly to Dover which would halt at Brush on request. Using the travel warrant issued to him by his adjutant, Wilson enjoyed the journey. This was the first time he had ever travelled on a train and he found it exhilarating, although the third-class carriage with its wooden benches was not very comfortable. But then, as a soldier, comfort was not something to which he was accustomed.

He enjoyed watching the countryside flash past the windows when not obscured by the clouds of smoke which billowed from the tall chimney of the busy little locomotive, which rattled and chugged along its rails at quite an alarming speed, stopping at small halts to drop off passengers and merchandize, and picking up others. At Faversham, which had a much larger station, the train stayed a while so that the boiler of the engine could be topped up with water, then they were off again. Not having the slightest idea how far Brush Halt was along the line, Wilson had arranged with the train guard to stop there and inform him that he had reached his destination.

Wilson alighted at the little station and looked about him. There was a single building comprising a ticket office and a waiting-room, with wooden benches and an empty fire-place. From behind the office there came a strange clattering sound, which he later learned was the new-fangled electric tele-graph. The only other person present was an elderly man in a uniform with the words 'Elam Valley Line' on his peaked cap, obviously the station master. On enquiring directions to Brush Hall, the station master, taking in the Lancer's uniform at a glance, nodded.

'You'll be wanting Captain Lindley, no doubt. You are in luck, young man, he's been at home for Christmas with all the family. And a right "do" of a party they've had and all. What with the dancing and a banquet. We had a special train laid on to bring

119

their guests from London and taken them home in the early hours of Christmas Day. Mind you,' he went on, 'that would not have been possible ordinarily, but seeing that Mr Farley owns the railway, he gets what he wants you see.'

Wilson was lost by this explanation, and asked who this Mr Farley was.

'Of course, you wouldn't know, young fellow. He's the Lady Emmerdale's new husband, Mr Jeremy's step-father. He's a railway tycoon, lives at the Hall. Of course the Hall belongs to the Lindley family, although I hear that Mr Farley is spending a lot of money on the house and the gardens. Needed it, too. The viscountess let the whole place go after her first husband, the colonel, died. Been a bit of a recluse since then. But she's a different woman now. Mr Farley has brought new life to the house and the village folk think the world of them both.'

The garrulous station master ran out of breath, and Wilson was able to ask directions to the Hall, and how far it was. The former was loath to cease gossiping, it was seldom he had such a captive audience, but finally he raised his arm and pointed to a lane which ran past the end of the little station yard where they were standing.

'Turn left out of the yard and follow the lane. When you get to the fork go left again, and it will take you past the Hall gates.'

Wilson saw where the station master was pointing, but the man then went on to talk about the Christmas party up at the Hall, and how the carriages had come to fetch the guests from the train. The corporal eventually managed to interrupt and thank the man for his help. Before he left he asked whether there would be a train back to London that evening, and was assured that there would be.

As he left the yard he could see the evidence of the presence of horses in the shape of a pile of dung left on the ground, doubtless from the carriages that had transported the guests to and from the Christmas party. Some party, he thought, and he was pleased to think that his journey would not have been in vain, and that he would find Captain Lindley at home. All seemed to augur well for the future, and he was sure that the captain would be able to help him.

He strode down the lane following the station master's directions. The air was crisp with wintry sunshine, and he was feeling almost his old self with little trace of his recent illness. His uniform met a few curious stares from the villagers that he encountered, to whom he offered a casual salute. He soon reached the entrance gates to the Hall and started up the curving gravelled drive, which finally debouched before the house. On the lawns beside the driveway stood a large colourful marquee which must have housed the Christmas party and before it was a group of people. Jeremy was easily recognized by his former orderly.

7

The marquee has been erected by swarms of work-men. A large four wheeled wagon had arrived with delicacies of fine meats, cold salmon and a variety of pies and game. Sweet-meats, fruit and confections were laid out to tempt the appetites of the guests. Serving men and girls were there to wait upon them. A small dais at one end of the pavilion was ready for the musicians who were busy sorting out their music and instruments.

A floor had been laid over the lawn for those who wished to dance, and was surrounded with small tables laid with fine damask linen and silver cutlery. Julian was busy bustling about with his usual energy ensuring that all was as it should be. Everything had to be just right and he was determined that nothing should go awry.

Alice, having made sure that the food and drink was up to the standard that she had demanded, retired to her bedroom, content to leave the final arrangements to her husband, to get herself ready before the first guests arrived. She had been up to London with Julian, who had insisted that she find herself the newest creation in gowns, and not to stint herself. He had bought her a lovely turquoise necklace – 'to go with your eyes, my darling' – as a

Christmas present, which she now fastened about her slim neck. Although she was nearing her sixty-eighth year, her skin was barely wrinkled, and her figure would be the envy of much younger women.

She was happy that she would have her family around her this Christmas, and that her eldest son was so visibly improving day by day, giving her high hopes that complete normality was a distinct possibility given time. So there was joy in her heart; who would have thought that in less than two years life could change so dramatically. She gazed out of the bedroom window. Even during winter the gardens showed care and attention with the promise of so much to come in the spring.

She heard footsteps on the landing and Julian's deep voice answering some query of Jeremy's, as the two men came to change into their dinner suits. The former stopped in the doorway with a look of admiration as, at a glance, he took in the elegant figure of his wife, now standing before the full-length mirror, smoothing the material of her beautiful gown. He crossed the floor quickly to grasp her hands and to hold her at arms length the more to gaze fondly at her.

'You look absolutely lovely, my darling, no one here tonight will look as beautiful, and they will know it. I am so proud of you.'

Alice blushed faintly at this praise, but knew it to be genuine and was happy to have his admiration.

'It really is a pretty dress and I love it. I want so much to do you justice and for you to be proud of me.' She kissed him gently on the lips. 'You had better get dressed before you get too enthusiastic!'

He turned to go to his dressing-room, pulling out his watch. 'The carriages I have ordered will be at the station in about an hour, that should be in plenty of time to meet the train. Thank goodness it is a fine evening, no snow as yet but there's a frost and that will help to make everything very festive, truly a traditional Christmas Eve.'

Gerald had gone up to his room earlier. He was now quite capable of dressing himself, albeit slowly, as if he found some difficulty in remembering the order in which to put on his clothes. Alice went along the landing and briefly knocking on the door, entered his room. She saw her son fingering his dress tie, holding it first one way and then the other, confused by its double ends. His mother gently took it from him and, first, fastening his stiff collar to its stud, she placed the tie around it and tightly knotted it, shaping the ends.

'How does that look? I think that you are very handsome. I seem to be surrounded by good-looking men.'

Just then, with a tap on the door, her younger son came in.

'Hello mother; I thought I'd just look in to give Gerald a hand, but I see that he is managing quite well himself.' Jeremy clapped his brother gently on the shoulder. Alice saw that her younger son was resplendent in his dress uniform. Colourful but smart with the blue monkey jacket buttoned at the neck, with twisted gold braid in three rows across his chest. He wore dark blue trousers with a pale blue stripe down the side of each leg.

Alice kissed him and stood back to admire him.

'You look splendid, Jeremy, all the ladies will be sure to fall for you, and I am so pleased you are wearing your medal.'

'You wait until you see the others, mother, they will

124

be even more resplendent. But there is only one lady whose eyes I want to capture. I hope that you will like Ruth, you must make much of her because I hope that she will agree to marry me. I am going to propose tonight if I can find the right moment.'

'I am sure I shall love her, I am quite confident that you have chosen well. I really do look forward to meeting her. Oh, it is going to be a lovely party, I feel that it will be a great success, and it was such a good idea of yours. Julian has enjoyed the organizing, and he is a stickler for doing things right.' She glanced out of the window. 'Goodness me, I can see the lights of a carriage. The first guests are arriving. Come on you two good-looking men, let us go down and greet them.'

She called Julian in the adjoining room. 'We are just going down, don't be long, dear.'

'Just coming, be with you in a minute.'

Then came hurried steps as he followed them down the stairs.

Alfred, the old retainer, who had looked after Alice these many years, and now doubled as a butler, looked very smart in new dress clothes. Flanked by two maids, brought in to help, he now stood ready to take the cloaks and hats of the arriving guests. As Alice and her two sons reached the hall Alfred was opening the front door to admit the first arrivals, who turned out to be the local clergyman, his wife and daughter. Whilst they were chatting in the hallway and being relieved of their coats, further carriages were heard approaching. Local squires and their ladies, the doctor from the next village and friends from the surrounding parishes. They were all escorted to the marquee where they were served hot rum punches. Gradually the numbers increased, and then, one after the other, the three specially ordered carriages arrived bringing those from the London train; Jeremy's fellow officers and the womenfolk, including Ruth, who had been escorted by Jeremy's colonel.

Amongst the last to arrive was Julian's old friend and fellow railway poineer, Robert Stephenson, who had been 'best man' at their wedding. They greeted each other as only good friends can.

By now the orchestra had begun playing and the marquee was thronged with those in evening clothes mingling with the officers in a variety of dress uniforms, resplendent in brilliant colour with gold braid and burnished buttons.

The whole of one side of the pavilion was taken up with long tables covered with damask linen cloths on which were displayed dishes and platters containing selections of delectable food. Pheasant, woodcock, snipe, together with salmon and trout. Delicate prawns in aspic and other tempting dishes. Two chefs stood ready to carve the best cuts from huge joints of beef and pork. There was an abundant choice for all to make the mouth water. Small tables were set at one end of the marquee to which waiters brought the food that the guests had chosen. The floor at the other end below the dais, on which the orchestra was seated, was left for dancing.

The whole of the interior was decorated in Christmas fashion with many coloured lanterns and candles, hanging from the tent poles and placed on the tables. Bunches of berried holly and mistletoe were hung about in profusion.

The splendid uniforms vied in colour and form with the elegant gowns of the ladies, whose low bodices and sweeping skirts made such a picture, a kaleidoscope of gorgeous hues of beautiful silks and satins. So that when some of them rose to waltz the flickering coloured lights caught the rich colourings of the dresses and uniforms, with the swirling skirts creating a rich rainbow and a mixture of all the colours of the spectrum.

The waiters had been busy offering some splendid wines, and later when the sweet-meats and fruit had been disposed of, liqueurs for the ladies and brandy for the men loosened tongues, so that the whole marquee echoed with cheerful voices and much laughter. Then, the orchestra changed the rhythm, and the lovely strains of Holy Night caused the guests to fall silent, such was the effect of the beautiful festive music. Further carols followed and everyone started to join in singing the familiar words, and suddenly, such was the prevailing nostalgia, to each came the spirit of the festive season; the joy and happiness that had always filled the hearts of mankind on the anniversary of the birth of Christ. Not only was it a wonderful party, but it was Christmas time. The true time for rejoicing and making merry.

The carols over, the orchestra rested awhile and took their refreshments, and it was noticeable that when they started to play once again for dancing, there was more verve and tempo to their music! Lines were formed for the Dashing White Sergeant and Roger de Covelly, and amidst the laughter and clapping the performers executed the turns.

When, at length, ordinary dancing resumed, Jeremy seized the opportunity to disappear into the house with Ruth. She was happy to be alone with him for awhile, away from the hurly-burly of the crowd. Jeremy drew the girl into Julian's study, and shutting the door, took her into his arms. She responded

127

readily to his kisses which soon became more ardent, and his hands began to wander over her lissom body.

She was a tall girl, almost Jeremy's height, but not lanky by any means, having a well-formed figure, a small waist and a high bosom. Her hair was dark and cut unfashionably short. She had full lips, a short straight nose and large and lovely hazel eyes. At length she halted Jeremy's wandering hands when they became dangerously provocative, and gasped, 'Please stop, darling, you are making it difficult for me. You know I want to as well, but not here, please.' She disentangled herself and rearranged the bodice of her gown which Jeremy had all but removed.

'Darling Ruth, will you marry me? I love you so much, and I want you so much, and I cannot be without you any longer. Even being near you makes me tingle with desire for you. It's hell not to be with you, please say yes.'

Ruth stopped him in mid sentence by kissing him on the lips.

'Of course I'll marry you, and how do you think I've been feeling? It is just as difficult for me. Don't you think I haven't wanted you just as badly? I cannot wait to be your wife. I want you to make love to me – but not like this.' She glanced around her. 'I am not so prim and proper, you should know darling, and I doubt whether I can wait for the marriage bed, but I have wanted and longed for you to ask me, and to be with you for the rest of our lives.'

'I hardly dare believe it, my darling. I have so much longed to hear you say that but hardly dared to think you would wish to marry me, and I became so jealous when I thought that you might prefer others. They had so much more to offer. I mean, look at me, not much future in the army with this arm, is there?'

Ruth put her fingers over his lips.

'Shh, my darling. You have always been the man for me since we first met this summer, and I swear that your poor arm makes you look so romantic. Actually, your Colonel Lester who escorted me on the train here, talked about you and your future in the regiment. I expect he guessed about you and me and was trying to be reassuring. He is quite a romantic under his gruff appearance. Thought the world of you and makes you out as quite a hero, and a credit to the Lancers.'

'That's decent of him, but what good am I with this gammy arm? I mean I can ride all right but nothing else. I could hardly hold the reins and use a sabre, could I? And I'm no good in an office doing paper work, which is what I have been doing lately, I get bored stiff.'

'No, I think that he has other ideas. He says that you are such a natural horseman that your talents should not be wasted. Perhaps he wants you to train the horses, or maybe, teach the new recruits. I don't know, but I am sure that he has something in mind. I don't think that he wants you to leave the regiment.'

'Then the sooner we get married the better, my sweet. I hope you will not want too long an engagement.' Jeremy groped in his pocket. 'As a matter of fact I bought you something to give to you tonight. You see I was determined to pluck up courage and propose to you here, it seemed such a proper occasion, but I was none too hopeful that you would accept me.'

Jeremy extracted a little chamois leather purse from his pocket and slid out a beautiful ring with a large yellow diamond surrounded by several smaller topaz stones.

Ruth held up her hands in delight.

'Jeremy, that is beautiful, it really is lovely, please put it on for me.' She held out her finger and he slipped it on, retaining her hand in his, and then kissed her, holding her to him for several moments.

Breaking away from his embrace, she asked, 'How did you know the right size? It fits so perfectly. No, don't tell me, I can guess, it's that young sister of mine. Anyway it was very clever of you, my darling, and I am so proud of it. Oh, it's lovely to see it sparkle in the lamplight.' She held up her hand to demonstrate.

'Come on Ruth, let's go and tell everyone. Oh, I am so proud, I cannot believe it, I really cannot.'

Ruth tucked her arm in his and they left the study and went back to the marquee. Alice and Julian were dancing together and, after a moment the couple managed to catch Julian's eye. Without a word Ruth held up her left hand where the ring sparkled. With a happy laugh Alice went up to them and put her arms around the girl, kissing her fondly, while Julian shook his step-son's hand asking his permission to kiss Ruth.

'This calls for an announcement, don't you think my dear?' Julian made his way through the dancers to the orchestra. They were just ending the piece they had been playing, and Julian bent over their leader and whispered in his ear. The musician nodded smilingly, and they finished their piece. Julian stood in front of them and raised both hands for silence. Beckoning his wife to bring the happy couple to stand alongside him, he made his announcement.

'Ladies and gentlemen, my friends, I have some very happy news to tell you, about which Alice and I are delighted and thrilled. It is my great pleasure to

130

announce the engagement of my step-son, Jeremy, to Ruth Broadhead, which has made both of us very happy indeed.' He paused as there ensued a loud outbreak of clapping and cheering especially from the group of fellow officers. Catching the eye of the head waiter he gestured to him, but the latter had already anticipated him and the glasses were being refilled rapidly. When there appeared to be a lull and everyone had been served, Julian raised his own glass.

'A toast, ladies and gentlemen, to Ruth and Jeremy, all our best wishes and congratulations for a wonderful future together.'

His guests responded vociferously, raising their glasses and cheering until the whole marquee resounded with their voices.

Alice suddenly felt a pang of guilty remorse. Caught up in the joyful response of their friends, she realized that Gerald would be bewildered at the strange hullaballoo that was taking place around him. She hastily looked about her to see where he was, and then, with some relief she spied him in the company of the clergyman and his wife. The latter knew all about her son's misfortunes and she thankfully realized that they were doing their best to explain the cause of all the rejoicing. It seemed that they were being successful for, even as Alice watched anxiously, she saw her eldest son begin to smile in understanding, and she blessed the good man and his wife for their intervention. Then she saw Gerald make his way towards his brother who, with Ruth, was surrounded by well-wishers.

Alice saw him push his way through the crowd to put his arms around Jeremy and hug him, and Ruth reach up to kiss him. Alice's cup was indeed full to overflowing with happiness. Life was good to her this

131

Christmas, any other time always the season of goodwill, but on this occasion especially so. Even if times were to become difficult in future years, this would be something that she would always have and nothing ever could take away or detract from the happiness that she was now experiencing. Julian sensed what was going through her mind, for he, too, had seen the episode of Gerald's understanding. He put his arm around his wife, hugged her and bending, kissed her on the lips. She clung to him for a moment murmuring, 'Oh darling, I am so happy.

Ruth radiated with delight, and, taking Gerald's arm, insisted that he dance with her as the orchestra struck up into a quickstep. With a little guidance Gerald soon caught the rhythm, and his legs responded to the music so that Ruth could relax and enjoy herself without having to lead him. Jeremy watched them, adoring the slim girl who had just agreed to marry him. He was deeply in love with her and was content that she could help his brother, who it seemed was already captivated by her. Gone was the shyness caused by his mental disability. That he was able to identify himself with others was a sure sign of the road to recovery, and Ruth had become another catalyst to this end.

Jeremy had not as yet mentioned the proposed dower house. Tomorrow they would walk to the top end of the park and show her where it would be built. No doubt the girl would have ideas of her own, but he was pretty certain that they would be the same as his. He day-dreamed of their future. A fine house and garden, perhaps two children running about in the park, making their own house in the hollow oak as Gerald and he had done.

Julian and Alice were dancing together too. Julian

was absurdly proud of all that he had achieved in so short a time. This party seemed a complete success with everyone in a festive mood. His wife was by far the most elegant woman present, who showed her breeding in every gesture. It was not so often that a self-made man such as he was able to achieve so much in so short a time. Everything that he had planned was coming about. It was almost too good to be true, and he must not tempt fate and ruin it all. He had not forgotten, however, his moments of passion with Fiona. That had been a fantastic union, but he had managed to subdue further thoughts of such sexual aberration . He had been a fool to jeopardize this new life that he had made, and nearly ruin his marriage by antagonizing his wonderful Alice.

Midnight was heralded by a roll of military drums, and Julian raised his glass.

'A very happy Christmas to each and every one of you, and may the spirit of goodwill always be with us.' He beckoned to the clergyman to join him. Standing beside his host he raised his right hand and gave the blessing to the now silent guests, saying a short prayer of thanksgiving for the birth of Christ.

The party continued almost until dawn, and then the arrival of the carriages that were to take those guests returning to London was announced. Finally the tired revellers, having collected their cloaks and congratulated their hosts on a wonderful evening, took their places in the conveyances and departed amidst shouts and calls of 'a happy Christmas'. Even as the last carriage left the drive their voices could still be heard singing carols as they departed.

Now that everyone had left, as the caterers cleared up their equipment and the orchestra put away their instruments, peace returned to Brush Hall. Julian thanked all those that had helped make the evening such a success, distributing largesse, and enjoying a final nightcap with them before they, too, left.

At last they retired to their beds as the frosty night gave way to a pale winter's dawn, to catch what sleep they could before the next day. Tired as they were the excitement of that evening made sleep a difficulty, and it seemed no time at all when they emerged from their bedrooms to welcome Christmas Day.

They had promised the vicar that they would all be in church for the Eucharist, for, as Alice had told them, it was the church's most important day, and it would not be Christmas without partaking in communion along with all the other village folk. The small church was already nearly full when they arrived to be escorted by the beadsman, holding his staff, to the family box at the top end of the nave. The whole congregation raucously joined in the familiar hymns and carols, and later, as they received their communion, the contrasting quiet made each realize how, through the ages, countless worshippers in this ancient church had filled it with an aura of tranquility and peace, leaving them with a feeling of humility.

The rest of the day was spent relatively quietly. They all trooped across the park to see the proposed site of the dower house which thrilled Ruth when Jeremy explained what Julian and Alice proposed.

'The next thing to consider is the wedding,' Julian remarked. 'Where and when? Do you wish to wait for the house to be finished?'

Jeremy looked at his fiancée quizzically who had the grace to look coy.

'I don't think that we can wait for that, for my part the sooner the better, and I have no doubt that Ruth feels the same.'

'Well then,' Alice ventured, 'how about the spring, say some time in April. They can call the banns any time now, so that's no problem, and you can live in the Hall until the house is ready. I am sure we can make provision in a wing of the house for you two.' She considered for a moment. 'Do you wish to be married at home, Ruth? It's the bride's perogative, you know.'

The girl shook her head positively.

'No, I don't think so. London is not really my home. Could I be married here in that lovely little church? After all, this is going to be my home, isn't it?' She looked at Jeremy for his approval, but Julian broke in.

'I do not think that anything could bring us more pleasure, do you my dear?' Alice was all smiles. 'That's definite then, you just leave everything to us.'

Ruth was quite overcome and embraced them.

'You are both very wonderful, thank you.'

The fine frosty weather continued into Boxing Day. This was the traditional day for giving and receiving presents and the gathering together of the family. It was also the tradition in the countryside to hold a meet of the hounds, and in this area the fox was the villain of the piece. But the Boxing Day 'meet' was not taken too seriously, as most members of the hunt were still suffering the aftermath of the Christmas celebrations. It was more the coming together of the local community, the rich and the poor, the squire and the yokel, the farmer and the shopkeeper. People from all walks of life met at the 'local', aptly named the 'Fox and Hounds', where before moving off, the hunt and the followers were provided with suitable drinks.

135

The party from the Hall arrived to find the road that ran past the inn crammed with people who had come to see the spectacle of the huntsmen in their vivid pink coats and the fine horses. They had to push their way through the throng in order to reach the inn door to find the inside crammed with more folk talking and laughing in the best of spirits. They were greeted vociferously, and seats were found for Alice and Ruth. The inn-keeper struggled towards them with a tray of drinks precariously held above the heads of the crowd.

Eventually, having refreshed themselves unstintingly, the riders managed, not without some difficulty, to mount their horses, the whips were cracked and some semblance of order restored as the hounds moved off followed by the straggling hunt. No doubt, were they to find a quarry, they would be led a merry dance, for the wily fox could probably sense the inebriated hunt, who would soon find the going too hard to cope with. Seldom did the Boxing Day hunt achieve a 'kill', but the exercise was for enjoyment, and the social contact, where all could meet on common ground.

In the past Jeremy would have been one of those on horseback, for both he and Gerald would have been in the hunt, but after Gerald's riding accident he decided that he would not have enjoyed it on his own, even had he been able to use his injured arm. And so they found a vantage point overlooking the area, and there they watched the hunt vainly chasing hither and thither as the hounds found a scent, lost it and then found another. Eventually they were lost to sight and the family returned home as the locals gradually dispersed.

Having eaten a cold meal they settled down in front

of a blazing fire and opened their presents which were wrapped in pretty coloured paper. A great contentment filled their minds and bodies as they relaxed in the comfort of their home.

It was not long however before Julian became restless, as he often did when he had nothing to do, and decided to take a walk in the garden.

'Come on Jeremy and you others, we cannot sit about all afternoon.'

As they sauntered past the now empty marquee, which was due to be dismantled the next day, they saw someone in uniform striding up the drive. As the stranger came nearer it was with startled surprise that Jeremy recognized him.

'Good lord, it's Corporal Wilson, my ex-orderly. What on earth brings him here?'

137

8

Jeremy walked across the lawn to meet the soldier, the others following him. Corporal Wilson threw up a smart salute and Jeremy held out his hand.

'Corporal Wilson, what brings you here? This is a surprise. The last time that I saw you was somewhere amongst the Russian guns. I am delighted to see you all in one piece.'

The soldier returned the handshake. 'Only got back from the Crimea a few days ago. I thought that I had better come and see you.' He eyed Jeremy's stiff arm. 'Glad you kept that, sir, it did not seem likely at the time when you galloped off holding the reins in your teeth. Lordy, that was quite a do. Didn't think we'd ever get out of that mess in one piece. There were a whole lot of us that were not so lucky. What a shambles!'

Jeremy became serious. 'Yes, we were very lucky. Come and meet my family, I am sure that they would like to hear your story and what happened to you.'

He introduced Julian and Alice. 'My mother Lady Emmerdale and step-father Julian Farley. My brother Gerald, and last but not least my fiancée Miss Ruth Broadhead. We've just become engaged.'

Alice welcomed the soldier warmly.

'Come along corporal, we were just about to have

a cup of tea, and you can tell us all that happened to you. We know that you had a terrible time, but, if it does not distress you we would really like to hear of your part in the battle. You have probably heard how famous you have all become. It seems it has been described as an epic battle and everyone has been talking about it.'

So Wilson told them everything that had happened and how fortunate his own escape had been. About the carnage and how he saw his friends lying on the battlefield mutilated and dying amongst the hail of cannon ball and grapeshot. Of the terrible winter and the shortage of supplies, and of the boredom at the siege of Sebastopol where he had been sent after the charge of Balaclava.

As they listened, only interrupting to ask a question here and there, the soldier continued. 'After the Russian surrender, and because of the sick and wounded, it was decided to evacuate as many as possible from the hospital, and send them home. My mates and I were part of a detail on one of the hospital ships to help look after them. Apart from the wounded there was a lot of disease and fever, and many of them did not survive the trip. We had to bury them at sea. Can't say that I liked the voyage. I mean fighting is one thing, but dying of fever is something else altogether.

'Of course my mates and I did all we could to protect ourselves. Having come that far we wanted to get home safely. We stayed on deck in the fresh air whenever we could, and washed in salt water, you know, all that sort of thing.' Wilson paused, frowning at some memory. 'There was a time when I thought I was a goner. Half way home, it was, when I took really sick. Couldn't leave my bunk I was that weak.

You know, sick and diarrhoea, if you'll pardon me ladies.'

'But you got over it all right,' Alice looked perturbed. 'I mean you are quite all right now, you look very well.'

'Oh yes, my lady, it only lasted two or three days. I reckon it must have been food poisoning, or something like that. Not surprising really, conditions aboard ship were awful. I'm all right now. Bit weak in the pins sometimes, with an occasional dizzy spell. But not surprising really. I was half starved by the time we docked in England.' He smiled. 'But it's grand to be home now, my mother and father weren't half glad to see me. I stayed with them for Christmas, then I thought I'd like to see how you fared, sir.'

'Good of you to come,' Julian interposed. 'But what of your plans now?'

'There's a train back to London, the chap at the station told me.' Wilson looked out of the window at the darkening sky. 'I had better get a move on or it will be dark before I get there.'

'No, you cannot go back tonight.' Julian spoke emphatically. 'I'll get Alfred to make up a bed for you in the servants' quarters. Besides I am sure there's much more to talk about, don't you think my dear.'

Alice nodded, rather reluctantly Ruth thought.

'Yes, of course, I will see to it.'

Jeremy got up. 'Leave it to me, mother, after all Wilson is still my responsibility, aren't you corporal? You don't mind messing with the servants, I am sure, and I know that they will wish to hear your story. Come on, I'll show you the way and fix you up with Alfred.'

When they had left the room Julian soon noticed the frown on Alice's brow.

'Something worrying you, my dear, you have become rather quiet.'

As Ruth guessed, her future mother-in-law showed little enthusiasm for the soldier to stay at the house.

'I am not sure Julian, I do not quite understand why Wilson should have become so ill on the ship and then made such a rapid recovery. It is almost as if he had contracted a fever, which seems quite likely in those prevailing conditions, but then he was sick for such a short time.'

'Well he seems well enough now, whatever it was. Oh lord, I hope he won't go down with it whilst he is here.' The implication of his wife's remarks suddenly struck him. 'Tell you what, I'll have a quiet word with old Doctor Armitage, not that he will knows much about fevers and suchlike; I do not suppose that he has much of that kind of illness to deal with here in the country.'

Jeremy chatted to his ex-orderly as he showed him the servants' quarters, and arranged with the old butler for a bed.

'And what of your plans for the future? Are you going to stay on in the Army, or have you seen enough of soldiering? There is talk of trouble in the Far East, and I expect they will be short of troopers in the cavalry, so no doubt the powers that be may change their minds about cutting down the size of the army.'

'Actually, sir,' Wilson answered hesitatingly, 'that was another reason why I came to see you. Of course I really did want to see how you were. I should like your advice, sir, I do not really wish to stay on in the cavalry. I should like a civilian job. But I really love horses, and so I wondered if you could help me.' He trailed off seemingly embarrassed.

141

'Of course, I'd be glad to be of any help I can. As a matter of fact I am in somewhat the same dilemma. With this gammy arm,' he patted the offending limb, 'I won't be a lot of good on horseback, but there might be an instructor's job available although no one has suggested it officially. If that did materialize no doubt I should need an assistant.' He considered the idea for a moment, then continued, 'On the other hand I have been thinking of the future. As you can see there is ample room here at Brush Hall for stabling and paddocks, and I might start either a stud or perhaps train race horses. That is all in the air, of course, but if I did that I should need help, and your experience might be invaluable.'

He introduced Wilson to the rest of the staff who were agog to hear about the trooper's part in the charge of the Light Brigade. He needed little persuasion and soon had his listeners hanging on his words as he told them, not without some embellishment, the more lurid aspects of the scene on the battlefield. Jeremy left him, smiling at the rapt attention that Wilson was receiving.

When at length the soldier ran out of steam, having answered innumerable questions about the fighting, he volunteered to help in the kitchen preparing dinner, much to the delight of the cook. Discarding his uniform tunic he set to work with a will. The staff were somewhat in awe, never having such close contact with a real soldier fresh from the battlefield; although they knew all about Captain Lindley's part in the fighting, it was not quite the same thing.

At dinner that evening Alice was still a little worried over the corporal's recent illness. When she asked Alfred how he was, she was even less reassured when told that he had been a great help to the cook in preparing the meal. But she kept her thoughts to herself, unwilling to upset the family, who had no such forebodings, and indeed had not given Corporal Wilson's illness further thought.

When, later that night as she lay beside her husband, Julian noticed her preoccupation and asked her if anything else was troubling her, she said, 'Oh dear, I was trying not to worry the others, but I am still very perplexed concerning that soldier. I cannot put it out of my mind that he could have contracted a disease on the ship, but how was it that he seemed to recover so completely when others died? I am probably being silly and imagining things, but there is the dreadful possibility that he could have had the cholera, and now he is in our house, touching things and breathing all over us. Julian, you will go and see Doctor Armitage tomorrow, won't you? And we must try and persuade Corporal Wilson to leave as soon as possible, as politely as we can.'

'I think that you are worrying unduly, my darling, but if it will set your mind at rest I will have a talk with the good doctor first thing in the morning, and tell him the whole story. If he does not know if it is possible for the corporal to still have the disease I am sure that he can find out for us.' He remained silent for a while deep in thought. 'Perhaps it might be as well to take what precautions we can, although it is probably too late. But as you say it would be best if he left first thing tomorrow. I'll make up some excuse, and have a word with Jeremy. I am sure we can come up with something to urge him on his way.'

Before breakfast next morning they discussed the situation alone with Jeremy, as Julian said there was no point in alarming Ruth unnecessarily. They explained his mother's disquiet over the corporal's sickness aboard ship and his seemingly miraculous recovery as the latter had recounted it.

'There is probably nothing in it,' Julian continued, 'but it is better to be on the safe side and send him on his way as soon as possible, and anyway there is nothing to keep him here now.'

Jeremy had long respected his mother's intuition, and her obvious worry had to be taken seriously.

'I had not given much thought to Wilson's illness, I was only glad that he recovered so quickly.' He frowned. 'I cannot believe that he could be contagious, he looks far too well, but I agree that it would be best for him to leave here as soon as there is a train available.' After a moment he added, 'I had promised to help him find employment as he wants to leave the army, and I cannot blame him for that after what he has been through. The best thing for him is to finish his leave with his parents and I will get in touch with him in due course when I have arranged something.'

His mother still looked anxious. 'But what if he is contagious, I mean, apart from us, won't he continue to mix with others including his mother and father? I should hate to be responsible should that be the case.'

'Don't forget, mother, he has already been with his parents over Christmas, so that won't make any difference. However, I suppose he should be isolated somehow, although, as far as I know the army medical people have never done anything like that before. Although, I suppose, they should be warned. Perhaps I should see the Medical Director and advise him of our fears, but quite honestly, mother, I do not think that you should worry about it.'

'The problem is,' Julian put in, 'we seem to be so ignorant about these diseases, let us hope that those

144

that should know can enlighten us. Anyway I'm going right away to see old Doctor Armitage and put him in the picture, and, yes, I think that you should go and see the army medical people, Jeremy. Even if they should poo-poo our anxieties, at least we have done our best and we cannot do more.'

Jeremy went off to find Wilson, who was enjoying a huge breakfast in the kitchen where the cook was fussing over him.

'You will be wanting to be off back to your parents no doubt,' he said, and without waiting for an answer went on, 'my step-father tells me there is a train to London in an hour's time, and I will see that the dog-cart is ready to take you.'

Poor Wilson was taken somewhat aback. He had not considered any immediate plans, only that he was enjoying the good food and attention given him by the Hall staff, and rather expecting that his sojourn there might be indefinite.

'Yes sir, I wil collect my things.'

'Good, but finish your breakfast first, cook would not want you to waste that good food, I am sure.' The cook was also taken aback by this rather abrupt dismissal of her new friend, but said nothing, adding more food to Wilson's already laden plate as soon as Jeremy had left the kitchen. Before Jeremy left he handed his ex-orderly two golden sovereigns.

'I expect this might be of some use,' he grinned. 'And my step-father says that you may travel free on his railways whenever you wish, and here is a note signed by him to that effect. I will be in touch with you as soon as I have something sorted out for your future. You are not to worry on that score.'

Well before the hour was up the corporal was on his way to Brush Halt, bemusedly wondering about

145

his abrupt dismissal as the dog-cart carried him down the lanes. It wasn't as if he had done anything wrong, he was sure about that, and Captain Lindley had been his usual friendly self. But it seemed as if he was not wanted any longer. Perhaps something else had occurred and he was in the way. After all he had arrived, as it were, 'out of the blue', and he could not complain at the friendly reception that had greeted him, or for that matter at their generosity. As if to reassure himself he felt the two gold coins in his pocket; good heavens, that should last him a while.

This made him feel better,and together with the captain's assurance about his future wellbeing, perhaps things were for the better; to say nothing of the large parcel of food in his haversack that cook had made up for him!

Later that morning Julian set out in his smart cabriolet which he had enjoyed driving so much recently. From its high seat he could see over some of the lower hedges and could view the countryside at leisure which was now in its winter guise. Later, when the spring came, the hedges would be full of new life and in bursting bud, and the wildlife would be emerging from their winter's rest.

Well wrapped up against the chill air he felt at ease with life notwithstanding a slight niggling worry and concern for Alice's foreboding. Doctor Armitage lived in the neighbouring village of Bishopsbury, some three miles beyond Brush. A widower for some years he was well respected, not entirely for his pills and potions, but for his care and the trouble he took with rich and poor alike. If he was able to alleviate the pain of those who suffered various ailments, so much the better, but it was his caring approach and kindness that made him popular, and he was never

146

too busy to give time to those who sought his help.

During the year that he had lived at Brush, Julian had met the doctor socially, but he had had no need of his professional advice as yet. In fact the latter had been a guest at the Christmas Eve party having known the viscountess many years. Even as Julian dismounted from the vehicle the doctor appeared at the door of his neatly kept house.

'Ah, I thought I heard that high stepping animal of yours. He is a fine animal and goes well with your smart carriage.' He stepped forward and caressed the horse's muzzle. 'What brings you here today, Julian? By jove, that was a splendid party you gave us the other night. Don't think I've enjoyed myself so much for many a year.'

'Thank you, doctor,' Julian shook hands, 'I have come for some words of your well known wisdom, seems there has arisen a possible problem.'

'Well let us go indoors, standing about in this chilly air won't do either of us any good. Tie your horse up to the gate then he can crop some of this grass, it needs cutting, save me the trouble!' He led the way indoors and into his study after Julian had hitched his horse to the railing.

The room was part study part consulting room with comfortable chairs and a desk strewn with papers, and shelves about the walls filled with books.

After seating his visitor in a large armchair, he busied himself at a cupboard. 'I have some really excellent Madeira wine here, you must give me your opinion. I always say it is never too early or too late in the day to enjoy a really good wine, helps to keep out the cold, too,' Passing a glass he filled his own, and Julian murmuring his thanks, tasted it.

'Ah yes, an excellent wine, you must tell me where

you obtained it.'

They talked wines for a moment or two, and then the doctor asked, 'What can I do for you, Julian? What's the problem?'

And so Julian told the good doctor about the visit of Corporal Wilson, and his story of the illness aboard the ship returning from the Crimea, and the subsequent concern that Alice had shown when she learned what had happened.

'So you can see why she is worried, and this was made worse when she learned that the good soldier had helped out in the kitchen. Frankly, I think that it is probably nonsense, nevertheless my wife has really been worried about it and so I thought that you could put her mind at rest.'

The amiable expression on the doctor's face gradually lessened as the story was told, and had changed to a frown by the time that Julian had finished. 'You say that these patients from the Scutari hospital had been in contact with cholera victims, and so probably carried it on to the ship with them?'

'That is what the corporal inferred. He said that there were several burials at sea, and undoubtedly these were the victims of disease and similar illnesses. He knew nothing officially, but from what he said there must have been quite a panic on the ship.'

'This is a very serious allegation, Julian. That ship should have been put in quarantine before she docked. Goodness me, if that had been yellow fever or smallpox, they would never have hesitated.' The doctor shook his head in dismay. 'This must be reported at once although it may well be too late. You see, cholera is not endemic in this country as such. We get occasional outbreaks in the slum areas generally due to primitive drainage. From the little that I know I believe the disease affects the bowels, so you can see how easily it could spread. And on board ship too,' the doctor shook his head in dismay.

He stood up and went to a book case, searched for a moment, and selected a slim volume. 'Here we are, I thought that I had something.' He held up the book. 'You can see from its size that not a lot is known about the disease.' He riffled through the pages and finally found what he was looking for. 'Yes, as I thought, bowel infection. Attacks the intestines. Short duration, patients rarely recover.' He read on for a moment. 'I am looking for something about the possibility of someone recovering and carrying the germs, but it seems that there is nothing known about that.'

'But can we dismiss the possibility that the soldier did have the disease, miraculously recover and still retain the infection?'

'My dear chap, so little is known about these so-called tropical diseases and their transmissable characteristics. No Julian, we cannot dismiss the possibility, but it is certainly something new to any medical knowledge and has not happened to date.' He thought for a moment. 'I think that even if there is nothing to this, we should inform the medical council of these events. And anyway, whoever allowed the disembarkation of that ship should be made answerable for their deplorable actions. Goodness me, I think that I could do with some more wine.' He refilled Julian's glass and then his own.

They were both silent awhile, each with his own fears and hopes.

'Would you like to come up to London with me, doctor? I think that this should be investigated more urgently than a letter will allow. My step-son talks about a Doctor Smith, the Director of the Army Medical Department, whom he had to see about his wounded arm.'

'I have heard of him too. If my memory serves me right he was the man responsible for establishing order out of the chaos in the Crimean hospitals, and was instrumental in sending that great lady, Florence Nightingale out there with her nurses.'

'If we could formulate a message emphasizing the urgency of the matter, I could telegraph it straight through from Brush Halt right away, and we could travel up first thing tomorrow morning, if you can spare the time away from your patients. I think that Doctor Smith will be bound to take note of any possible serious consequences, and should then be able to advise us. At least we will be doing something positive, and that will put dear Alice's mind at rest.'

'Right, let us get on with it.' The doctor reached for a quill pen, and after a moment's thought, wrote a message and carefully sanding it, passed it to Julian. 'That should do it, I think.'

'Yes, that is excellent. Thank you, doctor, I will send it straight away, and pick you up first thing tomorrow to catch the train to London.'

Arriving back at the Hall he told Alice about the doctor's reaction to what he had had to say.

'I am glad you saw him, dear, although we are no further forward as to whether that soldier was still contagious.'

'I expect that we shall never know.' Julian spoke confidently in an effort to allay any further worry. 'Perhaps Doctor Smith may know more. At least he should order an inquiry as to why the suspected cholera victims were allowed to disembark without quarantine.'

150

'Do you think that it might be a good idea to take Jeremy with you? He did meet the head medical man before, and will know the ins and outs of the department.'

Jeremy was glad to accompany them, and, early next morning having picked up Doctor Armitage, they caught the train to London. There, a carriage was hired, and Jeremy directed them to their rendez-vous. Julian's telegraph message had been received and they were taken without delay to Doctor Smith's office.

It seemed that they were expected, as they were escorted straight to the Director's office. The latter was not at all the sort of person that Julian had visualized. Tall and thin, almost cadaverous, he welcomed them with a kindly smile.

'Ah, young man,' he addressed Jeremy. 'We have met before if I am not mistaken. The gallant survivor of that infamous charge, who should have lost an arm. How are you?' He shook Jeremy's hand.

'Coming along slowly, sir, still very stiff though. Allow me to introduce Mr Julian Farley, my step-father, and Doctor Armitage.'

'Ah, doctor, I received your telegraph message, and I have instituted an investigation. Why those patients were allowed to mix with all and sundry I do not know, but I intend to find out. I gather that there is another matter that you wished to discuss, associated with it. I hope that I can help you, but you must understand that cholera is not an endemic disease in this country and we have much to learn, and much of what we now know we learned in the Turkish hospitals. But, please tell me your problem.'

Doctor Armitage related an outline of what had happened to Corporal Wilson on board the hospital ship and his seemingly miraculous recovery, and continued, 'You see his eventual arrival at Mr Farley's house seeking Captain Lindley, and later the disclosure of his mysterious illness aboard ship has caused considerable anxiety to the family with the possibility – although no more than that – he may have carried the germs of the contagion unwittingly. And I understand that before he told them of his illness he was mixing freely with the servants in the kitchen.' He turned to Julian, 'I think that covers the matter.'

Julian took up the story.

'My wife was the first to voice her apprehension. I have to admit that I had not considered the implications, but I could see that something was worrying her, and eventually she told me of her misgivings. If what she believes might be fact, my whole family is in danger, and now, I suppose, it is too late to do anything about it.'

Doctor Smith had listened in silence with a worried frown creasing his forehead. 'This is very serious, gentlemen. I cannot pretend that there is nothing in your misgivings, but there might well be repercussions if this soldier is indeed carrying the cholera germs. Frankly I have never heard of such a case, but that does not mean it is not so, there is evidence of other diseases being transmitted similarly. I fear that I cannot reassure you, but can only reiterate that such a case has never been reported.'

The others were silent awhile, each endeavouring to visualize the traumatic effects at Brush should their worst fears materialize.

The Medical Director continued, 'I should be greatly appreciative if you will keep me informed of any further developments. Should the worst happen and we do have an outbreak of cholera in your vicinity you will need help in succouring the patients and containing the disease. I can provide this immediately should it be wanted, but may God preserve us should that be necessary.'

They thanked him for his reassurance that help would be available should a crisis happen, but they bade him farewell with their fears only slightly mollified.

9

Dropping Doctor Armitage off at his house they returned to Brush Hall in the carriage with which the groom had collected them from the station. Alice met them in the driveway, an anxious frown on her face. Julian tried to allay her worries and repeated to her what the good Doctor Smith had told them. But he had to admit that in truth they were not that much wiser as to the possibilities of someone being able to carry the cholera germs, although being perfectly healthy in every other respect.

'You must understand, mother,' Jeremy put in, 'Doctor Smith has never heard of such a case before, although he had to admit that it is a possibility as it had occurred, he believed, with other diseases. But he thought it highly unlikely and we should not concern ourselves unduly.'

'I am sure that he must be right, and that I am a silly old worrier.' Alice was trying hard to believe the best. 'But, having said that, I still do not understand how your Corporal Wilson could have recovered so quickly. Very few got over it, I understand.'

Jeremy hastened to assure her that many patients did indeed get over the disease, but it took several weeks and certainly not days. 'I don't think that Wilson had cholera, it must have been food poison-

154

ing, or some stomach ailment.'

In spite of all their reassurances to each other they were a subdued family that night at dinner. The only cheerful one was Gerald who, of course, understood little of what their fears were about, and they did not think it necessary to enlighten him; rather that he should be in ignorance of the possible danger they might have to experience.

That night in bed Alice clung tightly to her husband as both lay in silence together. Then with a shuddering sigh she finally poured out her innermost worries.

'Oh darling, this last year has been such a wonderful time for us. It has been such a happy experience for both of us. Never did I ever envisage falling in love again. It would almost be ridiculous for me at my age even contemplating marrying again. And then you came into my life. You showed me that life was not over, you gave me new horizons and happiness, and you made my home alive again with my family around me.'

Julian held her hands and bent to kiss her eyes which were beginning to brim with tears. She responded for a moment returning his kisses, and in spite of her obvious distress Julian guiltily felt arousal beginning to take hold of him as her pliant body pressed against his.

She became aware of his excitement almost immediately and withdrew slightly.

'You see, my darling, I have this dreadful portent that, perhaps, our happiness was not meant to last. Such happiness at my age was too much to expect, and could be taken away as swiftly as it came. I should not grumble too much, I suppose, but to be shown such a wonderful year and then to lose it would be so cruel. I suppose that I have not deserved it. Make love to me, my darling; that will banish my fears, let us make love whilst we are able.' She thrust herself at him, curling her body into his loins and increasing the excitement that Julian made little effort to prevent.

He took her gently at first, and then, as Alice's passion became greater, with increasing fervour, thrusting into her violently and creating in her a response she had not known to have been capable of, indeed, as their mutual climax approached and the excitement in each increased, the explosion when it occurred was simultaneous to both. Alice had never known such sexual fulfilment; nothing like this. Love-making in the past had been satisfying and, she thought, complete. Her breathing had quickened to almost bursting point, and her whole body was responding with feverish groans, shuddering with the aftermath of her orgasm, almost threatening the cessation of her over-rapid heartbeat.

Julian too, when his mind finally cleared, had been lifted beyond the realms of sexual fulfilment. Even his torrid conquest of Fiona's virginity seemed to pale with the experience that his wife's passion had kindled in his body. Mutual passion and the need for each other under this dire threat to their existence had fuelled in both some extraordinary meaning to their love.

Sleep, when it finally came, was deep and dreamless, but not before they had again made love, albeit, without the same explosive mixture, but with a deeper and meaningful knowledge of their sexual fulfilment.

156

The knocking on their door became more insistent until Julian eventually became aware of the sounds. He opened his eyes. The room was still in darkness with the curtains drawn.

'Come in,' he called, at the same time reaching for his watch on the bed-side table. Rubbing his eyes, he had to look twice to make sure that the time was after eight o'clock. He was also surprised to see that it was Alfred, their old retainer, who had entered the room.

'Excuse me, sir. Shall I draw the curtains back?' Alice was awake too, and started to sit up, and then realizing that she had no nightdress, clutched the coverlet to her bosom.

'Cook is not well, sir, she has been vomiting. There has been a bit of an upset and I have been trying to cook the breakfast. I am afraid that I am not very good at it. I hope a boiled egg will be sufficient.' Having gained their undivided attention he continued, 'I asked Jenny, the kitchen-maid, if she could cope, but she said she did not feel up to doing anything. She complains of a headache.'

Their night of passion forgotten they looked at each other in consternation. Were their worst fears to be realized?

'All right, Alfred, I will get up and see cook. Perhaps she has eaten too much. You had better wake my sons. Do not worry about breakfast, we can manage.'

As Alfred reached the door, Julian said, 'Can you ask the groom to harness up Dobbin and get the cart ready? We must send for Doctor Armitage immediately.'

'Of course, sir, I'll do that first and then get the breakfast.'

As Alfred left, Jeremy appeared in his dressing

157

gown with Ruth just behind.

'I have just heard about cook. Do you know what is the trouble? It couldn't be something to do with Wilson, could it?'

The full implication of what he inferred immediately brought to mind their worst fears, and the silence that followed answered the question.

'Jeremy, get dressed quickly and take the dog-cart and fetch the doctor as soon as you can. The cart should be ready by the time you are dressed and you should be able to catch him before he starts his rounds. Bring him back immediately, tell him that cook is very ill.'

'I must go and see her and do what I can before the doctor comes,' said Alice, already starting to dress.

'Do you think that wise, dear, no point in taking further risks. I'll go, much better to keep everyone else away from her. Perhaps you could find some lysol and boil some water. I will try and clean up before the doctor sees her, Alfred said that she had been sick.'

Armed with bucket and brush, Julian made his way to the servants' sleeping quarters. Before he even reached the cook's bedroom, not only could he hear quite plainly her groans and the sound of retching, but the stench of vomit assailed his nostrils through the half-open door. Setting the bucket upon the floor, Julian soaked his handkerchief in the lysol, tying it around his mouth and nostrils in the hope that he would not inhale any germs that might be present. Probably a vain hope if it was cholera, but any precautions were better than nothing.

The woman was sprawled on her soiled bed, clutching her stomach as if she had the cramps. Even as he stood there another bout of vomiting cascaded into a chamber pot placed beside her on the floor. This appeared to ease her agony, and seeing Julian, she pleaded for a drink of water. She looked in a shocking state with sunken eyes, and her face had taken on a bluish tinge. Her voice was husky, and even to Julian, ignorant as he was of the symptoms, it was obvious that she was in 'extremis'.

Holding a glass of water to her lips, he watched her as she gratefully swallowed the liquid, and this seemed to ease her pain for the moment. Julian used this respite to start to clean up the mess that had splattered the floor and bed. He managed to remove the soiled sheets and, bundling them up in a heap, replaced them with bath towels, and then, finding a basin, replaced the half full chamber pot.

As he was doing this there was a knock on the half-open door. Alfred was reluctant to enter, wrinkling his nose at the smell of lysol which now permeated through the stink of vomit.

'Excuse me, sir, your breakfast is ready should you still want it,' intimating that it was indeed doubtful should he have any appetite after cleaning up cook's mess. 'And I am afraid that Jenny, too, has taken to her bed. Says she feels sick, and her stomach aches. I have taken some precautions and given her a chamber pot. I fear that I am not much good at nursing!'

'That's all right, Alfred. There is little point in taking any more risks than we need. I will do what is necessary until the good doctor comes, and then perhaps he will advise us for the best. Do you think that the girl is really ill, or copying poor cook?'

Before Alfred could reply, they heard the sound of Dobbin's hooves on the gravelled drive through the

159

window that Julian had thrown open in an effort to air the room.

'Ah, that will be Captain Lindley off to get the doctor, sir, he has not wasted any time.'

Jeremy had found the horse and trap ready when he arrived downstairs, and he soon had Dobbin trotting down the drive and along the lanes. He made good time to Bishopsbury, and finding the doctor up and about recounted what had occurred.

'Is your cook the only one that is ill? It could be just an isolated case of food poisoning.'

'I am not sure, doctor, someone did mention that the kitchen maid had a headache and did not feel up to much, but that was all. Maybe she is just apeing cook.'

Doctor Armitage looked grave. 'I think, Jeremy, we should be prepared for the worst, and then if nothing else happens we have at least done no harm. I think that we had better take up Doctor Smith's suggestion and ask his help. I expect that he will send us a nurse and give advice.' He considered for a moment while proceeding to pack his medical bag. 'I will write out a telegraph message and then perhaps you would be good enough to take it to Brush Halt and get it sent off right away. I can take my own conveyance to the Hall, I'll probably be there before you return.' He considered quickly, then wrote on a scribbling pad, tore the sheet off and passed it to Jeremy. 'That should do, short and to the point, I think. Right, I'm on my way, I will see you later.'

Jeremy unhitched Dobbin, and getting back on board, proceeded at a fast trot towards the Halt. Glancing at the doctor's message, he read, 'Our fears may have been realized, suspected outbreak of cholera at Brush Hall. Would be glad of your

160

proposed help, immediate, contagion difficult to isolate.'

'Oh God,' Jeremy felt a dread foreboding, 'spare our family from this dire calamity.'

He was not particularly religious, but as a fighting soldier he had always respected the hand of God that controlled each individual destiny.

He reached the station in good time and arranged for the telegraph operator to despatch the message, who, on reading it, wasted no time in doing so.

'I will stay here on duty seeing that this is an emergency, should you need me,' he promised.

Jeremy headed back towards the Hall dreading what might have occurred while he had been away. His thoughts were filled with visions of what the future might bring, and the danger that confronted his family. Dobbin knew his way home needing little guidance, and Jeremy allowed his eyes to stray. It was then that he appeared to have a double vision. There seemed to be two lanes, and the hedges to multiply themselves. He shook his head to try and clear it, when suddenly he was attacked by a ghastly feeling of nausea. Bile rose from his stomach and filled his mouth, and he only just had time to move his head before he was violently sick over the side of the cart. Dizziness filled his head, and his vision blurred even more as he continued to retch uncontrollably.

He was in a state of almost collapse as Dobbin, finding his own way home, arrived at the Hall and halted by the front door. Hawkins, the groom, hearing them, came to take the horse and cart to the stables, and saw Jeremy, seemingly collapsed half out of the vehicle. Calling out for help, he ran to assist, supporting Jeremy as best he could.

As he was attempting this, he was brushed aside,

and strong arms encircled the sick man and effort-
lessly lifted him down. Gerald had seen the arrival of
his prostrate brother, and had rushed out to help.
Somehow, on seeing the apparent desperate state of
Jeremy, something must have happened in his mind.
For suddenly he was half speaking and half crying in
a normal voice. Gone was the inarticulate stutter of
half formed words, slow and stumbling; the traumatic
sight of his brother had brought his mind back full
circle as it was before his accident.

Alice and Julian appeared in the doorway sum-
moned there by Gerald's cry. They stared at the latter
in amazement, not fully comprehending the reason
behind Gerald's sudden recovery. Then Alice
realized that it was Jeremy in her elder son's arms,
and that he was very ill. She ran towards them and
was shocked at the sight that met her. Jeremy was
barely conscious, his skin had taken on a bluish tinge,
and it was obvious that he was feverish.

Gerald carried his brother upstairs to his bedroom,
and Alice called, despairingly, for the doctor to come
quickly. One glance at the patient confirmed
Armitage's worst fears. Jeremy was now 'in extremis',
and there was little doubt in his mind, in fact in all
their minds, that this was the third case of cholera
which had struck so rapidly and so cruelly. For now,
Jenny, far from apeing the cook, was also near death's
door. Poor cook had become comatose, weak from
dehydration, and was delirious, becoming weaker by
the hour. Doctor Armitage could do nothing for her
except to make her as comfortable as possible, and
dose her with laudanum.

And now, while he ministered despairingly to
Jeremy, his thoughts were full of foreboding. There
was little he could do. The speed of the contagion was

so rapid, so horrific in the certainty of the outcome.

Ruth burst into the room, out of breath from running with a look of horror and foreboding in her face. She had been walking in the park when Dobbin brought her fiancé home, and then had encountered Hawkins who told her what had happened.

'Fair shook me, Miss, terrible state he was, half falling out of the cart, like. And then Mister Gerald picked him up in his arms, just as if he were a child, and carried him into the house,' Hawkins was garrulous in his story, but Ruth barely stayed to listen, and fled indoors.

Jeremy had, just at that moment, voided his bowels, and the stench pervaded the room. He groaned aloud as the cramps took hold of his limbs and he arched his back in pain. Ruth was at his side cuddling him in her arms, oblivious of the state that he was in, crying his name over and over again. He recognized her immediately and muttered, barely audibly, that she should not upset herself, he would be all right, and could he but have a drink of water, he was so thirsty.

The doctor nodded and added some laudanum to the drink, before he held it to to the patient's lips. Jeremy drank greedily and seemed more rested as the drug took effect. They could but notice the bluish tinge showing on the flesh around his mouth, and the beads of perspiration on his forehead which was feverish to the touch.

Julian, behind Ruth and Alice, could not remain idly by watching the sufferings of his step-son.

'I had better get something to clean up here,' he said, and went out, appearing a while later armed once again with buckets and cloths smelling strongly of lysol, and proceeded to mop up the filth. Then, with Gerald's help, he lifted the patient so that clean

163

linen could be laid beneath him. Gerald, now that he had recovered his power of speech, seemed inconsolable, continually beseeching that his brother should not suffer so, urging him to get better and recounting the happy episodes that they had shared as youngsters.

Alice seemed completely mesmerized by the turn of events. Almost incapable of believing that such a catastrophe should strike at her beloved son; this, hitherto so fit and healthy young man. How could this happen, and so suddenly, to a life that was so precious. To have survived the terrible battlefield and the ghastly hospitalization at Scutari only to be struck down through no fault of his own. At that moment, she, who had always believed in the goodness of God and His power over evil, began to feel that her faith had betrayed her. What had any of her kin done to deserve this ghastly fate?

Then she remembered what she had said to Julian the previous night in between their bouts of lovemaking. That their glorious life together this last year, which had brought so much joy to them all, was tempting fate, and that it had seemed almost too good to last. And now, it seemed, her forebodings were being justified. It seemed so unfair!

They spent the rest of the morning feeling frustrated and helpless. No one, except perhaps Gerald, could settle down to anything. Wandering about the house, Alice gazed at the familiar objects, associating each with some event over the past years. Happier times when her boys were growing into manhood. She now seemed resigned to the fate that had overtaken her family. She understood that only a miracle could save her Jeremy, and then, where would this dreadful disease strike next? God forbid that she should lose her other son, Gerald, now that he had recovered so suddenly from his accident. Perhaps she should not have brought him home from the institution. If she had left him there he might have been safe. So many 'ifs'. So easy to be wise after the event, she chided herself.

Doctor Armitage stayed with them the rest of the day, ministering to his three patients. Both the cook and the maid were slipping fast, both being in a semi-comatose condition, and he doubted if either would survive the night.

Jeremy seemed somewhat more stable, dozing in between further fits of retching made more painful now that his stomach was empty, and all he could void was bile resembling rice water which the laudanum seemed unable to stem, causing further dehydration requiring further liquid intake, creating a vicious circle.

Alfred and the house-maid, Sarah, attempted to produce a luncheon of sorts, although neither, with the fate of cook and Jenny in the forefront of their minds, put much heart into it. Neither were the others particularly interested in eating it. Although they made some effort, they could only toy with the food, having little appetite. Julian produced a bottle of brandy and persuaded the others to drink, perhaps in the vain hope that the alcohol might in some way sterilize further contagion by the vicious cholera germ. Julian, at least, did not stint himself, and a further bottle was produced and both Alfred and Sarah were persuaded to partake.

Later that afternoon, when the doctor had returned to his own home, promising to be back early next morning, a dog-trap brought the clergyman to the front door. Julian met him and suggested that although he appreciated the visit, the vicar should consider the danger of contamination were he to enter the house.

The good clergyman would have none of it.

'My job, good sir, is to visit the sick and dying, and my faith is in the Good Lord. Should He wish it, then so be it, I will be but dying in doing my duty. I should be failing in that should I allow any Christian soul to leave this world without His blessing in as far as I, poor wretch, can bestow it. Perhaps I can bring some comfort to them, perhaps I can lighten their failing spirits. God, you must understand, moves in the most mysterious ways, and although you and I may find it most difficult to understand, we have to believe that there is some reason to it.'

Julian could not argue with such beliefs in fate. To some the clergyman's words might sound portentous, but there was no doubt of the sincerity of this true man of God.

He brought him to Alice, and to her he brought a degree of comfort as he held both her hands and spoke to her.

'It is most kind of you to come, vicar, she said. 'I hesitate to say it, but I was really beginning to lose my faith in the rightness of God. It seemed so unfair to snatch away one's loved ones who had done no wrong. I can appreciate the perils faced by the fighting man, but this disease is so insidious, it does not discriminate, and there seems no rhyme or reason in its purpose. And its effects on its victims are so distressing.'

Tears filled her eyes and she broke into uncontrollable sobbing. The vicar put his arm around her and consoled her as best he could.

When she had recovered Julian invited him to see

the patients, offering a lysol-soaked kerchief to protect his mouth and nose which he declined, saying, 'I must keep faith in God and His purpose for me. It may well sound pretentious to you, sir, but if He wishes to take me from this life, then so be it. Also the patients may be very ill, but to see me, a man of God, protecting myself in such a manner would surely affect them adversely.'

They went first to see Jenny who lay on her bed moaning in a semi-conscious state induced by the laudanum which the doctor had administered. The flesh of her face was now becoming blue in colour, and her eyes were sunken into their sockets. Her breathing was shallow and she seemed very close to dying. The vicar appeared shocked. He had never before seen a victim of cholera, and the sight of Jenny had a profound effect upon him. Shaking his head in dismay he mumbled a short prayer, and made the sign of the cross over her and then hastily turned away.

'Poor girl,' he muttered, 'what a terrible thing this is.'

'Would you rather not see the others? I can well understand how you feel,' Julian said.

They were outside cook's room, and after hesitating, the clergyman went in, only to come to an abrupt halt just inside the door.

'I rather fear that I am too late.'

Cook lay on her back, eyes wide open already beginning to glaze. A trickle of vomit dribbled from her open mouth with its grimace of pain still evident.

'Dear God, receive this thy good servant into your loving care out of this troubled world.' The vicar made the sign of the Cross, and kneeling on the floor said a further prayer for the dead.

'Not a very pleasant way to die, vicar.' Julian tried to keep the tremor out of his voice. This first death was so sudden and traumatic, and he knew that this would not be the last. What of the others? In his heart he feared that nothing was going to stop this spectre of death invading his whole household. What was to be the end of it all?

'I must see your step-son. Please show me where he is.'

They found Ruth still with Jeremy, who had also been dosed with laudanum, but was still conscious although racked with pain from the cramps in his limbs, and was tossing and turning in semi-delirium. He seemed to recognize his visitors however, for, grimacing with pain he smiled weakly trying to say something only to collapse with the effort. The vicar urged him not to exert himself and attempted to comfort him. As he gave Jeremy the Blessing, the latter closed his eyes as if the words brought some peace, and then he seemed to lapse into unconsciousness, whereupon Ruth, kneeling beside the bed, started to weep bitterly.

As they descended the stairs, there was a crash and the sound of breaking crockery. The disturbance seemed to originate from the kitchen area. Alarmed, Julian hurried in that direction closely followed by the clergyman, only to halt outside the pantry. Upon the floor, amidst the shards of broken china and upset cutlery, Alfred lay sprawled. It was evident that a bout of sickness had suddenly overtaken him as he had vomited on the tiled floor, and had collapsed in pain, obviously unable to control his limbs, scattering the contents of the tray that he had been carrying.

As Julian hesitated, not knowing what to do first, hurried footsteps brought an ashen faced Sarah to the door. Kneeling beside Alfred she attempted to roll him on to his back calling for the others to help.

'We must get him to his bed, we must do something.'

Julian bent to help, wondering inwardly if it really was worth the trouble. If, in fact, anything was worth further trouble!

If they were all to die, why not where they were. In any case who would be left to assist the last to go! He shook himself trying to dispel further morbid thoughts. They must have help, and soon. By now Doctor Smith would have received the telegraph message that Doctor Armitage had dispatched with Jeremy, and would send help. He hoped that his stepson had in fact sent off the message before he became ill.

The clergyman was obviously thinking along the same lines. As he bent to assist Julian to lift the unconscious Alfred, he said, 'I think that I am too old to do this, we shall have to get help. You need nurses too. I fear that I am not strong enough to help you get him upstairs.'

'No, of course not, we'll put him on the settee, here, in the hall. Sarah, see if you can find Mister Gerald and ask him to come and help us, please.'

While they waited, Julian related to the vicar their visit to Doctor Smith in London. 'He will have received the telegraph message by now, so let us hope that he will act upon it without delay. It would not be right to ask the help of the village folk for the disease is too contagious. I might ask Hawkins for help, but I hesitate to risk any further victims. No, this house must be isolated, this evil must be contained and destroyed.'

Julian became very agitated at the thought of this

cholera spreading far and wide, and was adamant that Brush Hall should be the stopping point. 'It must end here, vicar.'

The latter considered this for a moment, and then said with a wan smile, 'But how about myself? I cannot remain here, I must see my wife. If I am contagious then she may well become so!'

Julian hardly wished to remind the vicar of what he had said earlier; how that his faith would protect him. Instead he suggested that he should see no others and neither should his wife for a day or two.

'You must understand, vicar, that the soldier who brought this plague into the house was here for less than twenty-four hours, and cook was ill two days later followed by Jenny and then Jeremy. And so it looks as though it takes only two or three days from contact to the appearance of the first symptoms. I should say that if both you and your wife could isolate yourselves for that time, and if nothing further occurs, you will probably consider yourselves unaffected. Let us pray that this is so.'

'Yes, I will certainly do that, but how about the good doctor? He will be visiting his usual patients I suppose. May not he infect them all, if this cholera spreads from contact?'

'I should think that he has already considered that possibility, after all he must have known the risks far better than us.'

Alfred chose that moment to come to his senses, and them promptly vomited all over the floor. Just as this happened Gerald appeared on the scene. Together they got the sick man upstairs to his room, and removing his soiled clothes did their best to cleanse him.

Meanwhile Sarah seemed to have disappeared.

170

Julian had forgotten all about her while he had been talking to the clergyman. Then they heard a cry from Jenny's room, and rushing in to see what had happened, they saw that the girl had died. Sarah was sitting on the bed beside her, distraught and holding her head in her hands, looking far from well herself, rocking from side to side.

'Oh what is to become of us? Poor little Jenny who would never harm anyone, and now she's gone. It will be my turn next, I know it will. What shall we do?'

They tried to calm her, and Gerald led her out of the room. They covered Jenny up and said a prayer over her.

'I think that I had better find my wife and tell her what is happening,' said Julian. 'Everything is occurring so quickly. Come along, vicar, I am sure you would like a brandy, never mind the time of day!'

They found Alice comforting Ruth, trying, perhaps not very successfully, to reassure her. One glance at the faces of the two men as they entered the room banished her hopes. She rushed up to Julian who clasped her to him as he told her about cook and Jenny, and how Alfred had become sick.

So much had happened already they seemed to have lost all sense of time. No one felt any desire for food, even had there been someone to prepare it. But the brandy found ready acceptance, helping them in some small way. Julian's thoughts were in turmoil, it seemed as if the whole household was under sentence of death. The thought of losing his beloved Alice was unbearable. Perhaps they could die together; life alone was now unthinkable.

The clergyman departed to his own home with mixed feelings. He was loath to abandon this stricken family, but eager to return to his wife. He wondered how he would cope with the burials that would be inevitable over the next day or two. He knew there would be more deaths. Jeremy Lindley had the look of death already, and poor Alfred was rapidly sinking into a coma. Sarah, the housemaid, was behaving very oddly, and Ruth, Jeremy's fiancée, in refusing to leave him seemed destined to become infected.

Nothing further occurred that evening, and finally Julian persuaded Alice to come to bed. Looking in on Jeremy they found Ruth still with him, bathing him with wet compresses, and whispering her love for him, trying to instil in him the will to survive.

Gerald has already retired. He now seemed quite normal, although he had become very quiet and said very little. Alice clung to her husband with a desperation borne of despair, cursing the cause of the disaster and the soldier who had come to their house. There was little to say, as Julian tried to find some words of comfort.

Eventually they slept, exhausted by mental anxiety. The sun was well up and it was its winter rays that finally woke Julian. No one had disturbed their sleep, and no sound was heard as the house slept.

Then, Julian thought that he heard the sound of horses' hooves and the crunch of wheels on the gravelled drive. Alice was still sleeping as he jumped out of bed to look through the window in time to see a cloaked figure emerge from a carriage and hammer on the front door.

The sound seemed loud in the sleeping house as Julian hurried downstairs to unbar the door and admit this early visitor.

Throwing back the hood of her cloak, Fiona reached out to grip Julian's arm.

'My dear, I came as soon as I heard from Doctor

Smith.'

Julian could hardly believe his eyes. It seemed that here was the veritable angel of mercy. The same angel that had succoured the ill and wounded at Scutari.

'My dear,' he finally managed to croak, 'oh how glad I am to see you.'

'How bad is it, Julian, is Alice all right?'

Whatever else she was about to say was interrupted by a piercing shriek, a wail of utter despair that echoed through the silent house. Quickly recovering from this unearthly sound, Julian rushed up the stairs rapidly followed by Fiona. As they reached the landing, the door to Jeremy's room was flung open and Ruth, still in her day clothes, charged past them and, running down the stairs, disappeared through the still open front door.

After a moment's hesitation, Julian turned to follow the girl, while Fiona hurried into Jeremy's room. Julian could see Ruth haranguing the driver of the carriage that had just brought Fiona. Then he saw the girl get into the conveyance which was rapidly turned around. Even as he approached, it broke into a fast trot and disappeared down the drive.

Returning, Julian found the others standing just inside the bedroom door watching Fiona as she examined the recumbent form on the bed. He saw her draw her fingers over the staring eyes, closing the lids. And he knew, as did both Gerald and Alice, that his stepson was dead. This brave man who had defied the odds on the battlefield, had fought the enemy and endured the awful and horrendous conditions of Scutari hospital, had finally succumbed to a more deadly foe, an enemy against which there was no weapon.

173

The ensuing silence was shattered by a dreadful, maniacal cry. Gerald lifted his head and howled like a wolf in the fastness of the forest.

'Jerry, my little brother, oh Jerry!'

And as he turned to face the others, they saw the mad gleam in his eyes, his damaged brain succumbing yet again to the injury he had previously suffered.

Julian went to him in an attempt to console him, but with another demented howl, Gerald shook him off, stumbling out of the room. They heard him clatter down the stairs, and a moment later a door banged somewhere in the house.

'My God, is that the gun-room? What is he doing?' Alice was beside herself and becoming hysterical. Then they heard Gerald open the front door. Rushing across to the window they were in time to see him stride across the drive, holding Julian's sporting gun under his arm, and make his way into the park. 'He's going to do something awful, oh, for pity's sake stop him.'

They rushed towards the stairs, Alice leading the way, panic stricken so that she barely knew where she was going in her haste to catch her son.

And then, in her frantic hurry, the inevitable happened. She was still in her night attire covered only in a long dressing gown. Her foot caught in the hem of the garment, and missing a stair tread, she stumbled and fell, tumbling down the remainder of the steps and coming to rest at the bottom, to lie inert with her head twisted in a grotesque fashion.

Julian was beside her within seconds, and cradling her head, he tried to revive her, murmuring endearments, and begging God to save her. Then Fiona was beside him. One look at the stricken woman and she

174

realised that the fall had broken Alice's neck. She was quite dead with no hope of recovery.

Julian must have realized this too, for, with tears streaming down his face, he lifted his wife into his arms and stumbling back upstairs laid her on her bed and buried his head in her bosom. After a while he asked, in a stricken voice, 'Oh God, what have we done to deserve this? Why have you taken away all that I hold most dear? Why should I be left? Why Alice, who knew no wrong?'

Fiona tried her best to console him, but he would not be comforted.

'This filthy plague. Last week we were a happy family all together, and then that man brought this filthy disease to this house. Is there to be no end to the dying?' He looked up at the girl. 'It's got to be stopped. There is only one way to destroy this evil, and it's got to be now.'

He rose from the bed, tears still streaming down his cheeks, and as he was leaving the room he turned to Fiona. 'See if you can find Sarah, she is the only other person left. Take her with you and leave this house.'

'Julian, what are you going to do?'

Without answering he left the room, and as he did so the faint sound of a gunshot could be heard from across the park, somewhere near the old hollow oak tree.

Julian hurried to the back of the house, where, in a shed, he found what he was looking for. Two cans containing lamp-oil were stored there, and, without hesitation he carried them back with him and took them upstairs.

Fiona had searched vainly for Sarah and could not find her anywhere, so came looking for Julian. She

175

discovered him splashing the oil over the dead bodies of the servants, over the furniture and bedding, soaking the bedrooms. In consternation she followed him, vainly beseeching him, only to be totally ignored, and finally she watched him carefully soaking Alice's bed, and then realized his ghastly intent.

As he poured the last of the oil on the surrounding carpet, Fiona could hear him muttering to himself, and could just make out what he was saying.

'Fire to purify and destroy this evil. Everything must be burned.' And then, half sobbing, 'My wonderful Alice, how can I continue to live without you? All this desolation, my life is forfeit, here, where we first loved so little time ago. I will finish it all, and join you in paradise.'

Fiona realized that Julian was half demented with this tragic loss. He was not in his right mind for she could see that he meant to end his own life in the arms of his dead wife.

'Julian,' she tugged at his arm, calling to him until at last he turned towards her, his face a mask of stricken desolation that, for a moment, she was too aghast to continue. 'Julian, my dear, you must not do this. There is another you must think of now. Look at me, please.' She placed her other hand upon her stomach. 'There is new life inside me, your child who must have a father, if only for its sake you must strive to put this all behind you and live.'

Julian's glazed eyes took in the rounded form of the girl's abdomen. So much had happened since she had arrived so short a time ago, that he had not taken in the fact that the girl was now several months pregnant with his child. For a moment his eyes closed as he understood what she meant, but then the stricken look returned.

'No, I must end it all, I cannot live without my Alice,' Shaking himself free, he took up a taper, intent on his awful mission.'

Understanding that she alone could not stop him, Fiona fled the room intending to find help, leaving him to his dreadful task. Deliberately he lit the taper and went to the servants' quarters. It was here that he would start the all-consuming fire. With the bed-clothes around the body of cook well alight, he made his way to the other two rooms, setting fire to them before going to Jeremy's room where he continued his desperate act.

Then he went to his own bedroom where the body of his lovely wife lay on their marriage bed, her sightless grey eyes still staring. Overcome with grief, he flung himself beside her, dropping the still lighted taper on the oil-soaked carpet.

The flame spluttered for a moment, and then, slowly at first, the fire took hold. Oblivious to the holocaust that he had created, he lay beside his dead wife, dementedly crying, 'Oh Alice, my darling, I will never leave you.'

Then rough hands seized him and dragged him off the bed, endeavouring to make him stand upright. Fiona had found Hawkins and the old gardener running towards the house, alerted by the smoke and flames issuing from the upper storeys. Together with Fiona they struggled with the demented man, who now fought them with demoniacal fury, defying their efforts to rescue him from his own fate.

The struggle continued as Julian fought them, and for a moment it looked as if their efforts would be in vain, and they would have to save themselves from the spreading flames.

In growing exasperation, Hawkins, a one-time

prize fighter, decided to settle the issue, and a perfectly timed short jab found Julian's jaw, causing him to subside unconscious upon the floor. Together, half carrying, half dragging his limp form, they hurriedly made their way out of the house, not pausing until they were a safe distance away. There they dumped their master on the ground and turned to see the upper part of the Hall engulfed in flames.

EPILOGUE

Back in the derelict yard we stared at each other in utter bewilderment. Guy was the first to speak. 'Well, there's your railway all right, or whatever is left of it. It must have been shut down a considerable time ago. Before we came to Brush at any rate, not that that means much. We can find out more about it at the local; there's bound to be some people in the village who remember it.'

'That is all very well,' Diney joined in, 'but what about that?' She pointed at the wheel tracks and the pile of dung.

We gathered round the marks in the snow, and Julia, who had often taken part in driving classes at various county shows in the past, and was something of an expert on wooden-wheeled carriages, was quite sure that the tracks were made by the carriages we had seen the previous night, or something very similar.

'Then, how do you explain that? If I alone had witnessed last night's event you would have laughed and told me to lay off the vino; but we can't both have had hallucinations, surely?' I tried to think of some other explanation, nothing came to mind, and the others were equally puzzled.

'We should have a record of this,' Guy remarked,

'come a thaw the tracks will disappear. Let's go back to the house and get my camera. I know that it is still loaded, and then we can photograph the whole place including the original track. People will have to believe us then.'

We piled into the car, careful not to confuse the cart tracks, and, returning to the Old Grange, Guy collected his camera.

About an half hour later he had taken photographs of the mysterious carriage tracks and the prints made by the horses' hooves, together with the pile of dung. With the converted station buildings in the background and several shots of the old rail track, Guy made a composite collection of photographs which would portray the presence of the mysterious carriages and their horses. There were some human prints in the snow as well, but these had been well smudged and might have belonged to anyone.

It was now midday, and, as Guy remarked, the pub would be open. 'We could have a drink and ask Nobby, the landlord, about the old railway.'

Julia and I were introduced as we settled down in the 'snug' but could hardly hear ourselves speak. Everyone was celebrating Christmas Day, each in his own fashion. Carols were being sung somewhat raucously, and others were shouting in order to be heard. Eventually Nobby Crick, the landlord, had a free moment to chat with us.

'Tell me, Nobby, who would know anything about the old railway up at the halt? My friends are very interested in its history. Do you know when it was closed down?'

'Before my time, commander; must have been before the war or just afterwards. It was shut down when I took over here, and that is over ten years ago now.' He stopped to think, absent mindedly scratching the back of his head. 'Tell you what, though, old Ben over there works on Gedge's farm, he's lived here all his life. He should know if anyone does, knows the whole village, he does. Tell you some tales he can, never knew a bloke for such gossip! I'll fetch him over, no good calling in this din!'

So saying the landlord went over to the smoke-room where old Ben could be seen gossiping to a group of labourers.

Presently we saw old Ben leave the group with whom he had been talking and make his way towards us. He was the typical gnarled countryman, face reddened by the winter winds and about sixty years old.

'Draw him a pint of what he likes, Nobby,' Guy said to the landlord.

'Begging your pardon, commander, but a tot of rum is his tipple.'

'Quite right, too,' the naval man replied.

'Afternoon ladies and gents,' Ben touched his cap with his forefinger, but failed to remove it; probably never does I thought. Nobby introduced us and went on to tell the old man why we wished to talk to him.

'You see, Ben,' I said, 'we found this old station last night in the snow, and it appeared to be still in use. But this morning in daylight we found it derelict.' We had decided not to tell the old man about the carriages and the strange people. 'Do you know much about it? Has it been shut down for long, and where did the line go?'

'Ahh. Well it was closed at the beginning of the war, 1940 or thereabouts. A new line was running to Dover at that time, and they decided that this was not economical, and they could put the steel lines to

181

better use. Guns and tanks I wouldn't be surprised!'

'But surely, Ben, this was a bit out of the way to have a railway? I mean Brush is something of a backwater, probably more so in those days,' Guy said.

'Ahh, there's more to it so I've been told. A Mr Farley, who came from the north, he was what they called a pioneer or some such thing, he built railways all over the place. Seems he thought he could make more money down here; you know carrying the mail and that sort of thing.'

The cacophony, that had assailed our ears and had made us almost shout to be heard, suddenly died down as the singing stopped, and many of those making the noise left the inn amidst well wishing farewells.

We could now speak normally and Guy took the opportunity to order another round including a further tot for old Ben.

Raising his glass in salute, Ben continued.

'My family have lived at Brush a long time, so most of the gossip gets handed down from father to son. Well anyway, my great grandfather was gardener up at the Hall, about to retire he was when this Mr Farley arrived on the scene.' He took another sip of rum which was certainly helping to loosen his tongue.

'The lady, who was living at the Hall, was a widow woman. Her husband was a famous soldier, Lord Emmerdale, who died soon after the battle of Water- loo from wounds. I heard the tale that this chap, Farley, fell for the viscountess. Swept her off her feet, and then married her. Spent a fortune on the house, all the money he was making out of his railways.'

'That would be the old ruin at the foot of the park,' Nobby, who had been listening with us to Ben's tale, put in. 'Got burnt down years ago, it did. Proper

182

eyesore now, isn't it, Ben?'

'Yes, old Colonel Fortescue who owns it won't have it touched.' Ben turned to us. 'Best you go and see him. He's some relation to the old viscountess, and the last of the family. Lost his only son in 1940. But you go and see him. There's more to the story of Brush Hall. I do know, though, that my great grandad helped to rescue that Mr Farley when the Hall was on fire.'

'Oh, I know who you mean,' Diney exclaimed. 'He's the old man who lives by himself in the dower house at the top end of the park. Owns all that land. He was in church this morning. Typical army type. You remember, Guy, we've met him several times.'

'Yes, he's something of a recluse. I wonder whether he would talk to us. I think we have stumbled upon something very mysterious,' Guy grinned at us.

'Come on chaps, time to go home, it's lunch time. It's been very nice talking to you, Ben,' Diney took the old man's hand and shook it.

Ben put his finger again to his cap, 'And a very happy Christmas to you ma'am, and to all of you. It's been a pleasure talking to you.'

'And to you, Ben,' we all said.

'Only a cold buffet,' Diney told us as we piled into the car, 'proper dinner tonight, real Christmassy sort, and you are all to change. We've asked the vicar and his wife, they are alone this year. You met them this morning so it won't be too sticky for you.' Diney laughed as Guy pulled a face. 'They're nice people and get on well with the village folk. I think that Guy gets a bit nervous in their company, has to mind his language, don't you, darling?'

'Oh they're all right, some wine will loosen their tongues I've no doubt, and we can tell them of your

183

experiences last night. Talking of that, perhaps we should contact old Colonel Fortescue tomorrow, see if he can see us some time.'

'He might be at the Meet,' Diney said, turning to us. 'We always have the Meet at the pub on Boxing Day. It's been held there since time immemorial. One of our traditions I suppose. I think that the Colonel was Master of the local foxhounds once.'

The cold buffet turned out to consist of a magnificent game pie with all the bits and pieces that go with it, and was followed by a real trifle. Needless to say the afternoon was spent lazily, so replete were we.

However, having had a good snooze, I began to feel restless and decided to go for a walk.

'Don't include me, darling, I am far too lazy,' Julia murmured. 'You go ahead, but don't get lost, the daylight will soon fade.'

I wrapped myself up and, borrowing a walking stick made my way towards the village. Some instinct seemed to guide my footsteps, for, after about twenty minutes or so of brisk walking, I had left the village behind soon to find myself approaching the gates of an estate.

The brick pillars that had once supported the wrought iron gates were crumbling and covered in ivy, and one of the gates had fallen from its rusted hinges and lay in the long grass at the side of what had once been a wide driveway, but which now could hardly be discerned; it was so festooned with weeds that it had become part of the parkway to which it adjoined.

My instinct again led me forward as I followed the curve of what once was a wide drive. This eventually arrived before the remains of what must have been a fine house. Only the lower walls remained now. Some broken blackened timbers still arched into the sky, but nature had taken over and young saplings and bushes seemed to soften the bleak ruin that confronted me, and no doubt in the spring it would be clothed in foliage and blossom similarly masking that which the snow was now hiding.

This then must have been the old Brush Hall where Ben's great-grandfather helped to rescue Julian Farley. I wondered what lay behind these happenings of some hundred years ago. Hopefully Colonel Fortescue might enlighten us, because here, I felt, was a mystery hiding some tragedy, and I could not but help think it might have some connection with the funny little train with its travellers that had seemed so real to Julia and myself in the snow on Christmas Eve.

I poked around a bit further but there was little else to see as everything was coated with snow. The remains of a walled garden were discernable, but the rest seemed a wilderness. One could see, however, where the parkland started with its great trees dotted here and there.

As Julia had predicted, the light was fading fast, and I had to walk quite quickly to reach the Old Grange before it had gone completely.

'Hello, old boy, we were thinking of sending out a search party, thought that you might have got lost!' Guy and the others were still sprawled around the fire, but now there was tea and crumpets, and a fine cake decorated with a Father Christmas and his sledge upon the top.

Come and get warm, darling, and have some tea whilst its hot.' It was a very happy little party, almost a family affair since we were such old friends.

'Where did you walk to?' Diney asked as she poured

out my tea.

'I think I found the old Hall, or at least what's left of it, and that's not much. You know, the place old Ben was talking about.'

'Yes, we know it but never took much notice, I don't know why, never asked I suppose. Didn't even know it belonged to old Fortescue. We rather seem to mind our own business. Being relative newcomers I suppose we tend not to listen to the gossip! But, you two have stumbled across a mystery, and I have to admit that it grows curiouser and curiouser, and I cannot wait to find out what Fortescue has to tell us.'

We had been warned about dressing for dinner and had brought evening clothes. It may have been an old world custom, but it was so appropriate for Christmas, and the season where goodwill should prevail.

The vicar and his wife arrived soon after Julia and I came downstairs, and Guy busied himself serving a hot rum punch. The talk was quite general to start with, and the clergyman vouchsafed the opinion that there was a thaw coming.

'It seems much milder this evening and there is a mist rising in the meadows. I shouldn't be surprised to see some rain or sleet before morning.'

'Then there may be some hunting after all tomorrow, for what that's worth on Boxing Day.' Guy was not a hunting man, but enjoyed the social part of the Meet. 'Must have a Meet on Boxing Day, it's the tradition here, never missed one for donkey's years, I am told; but the snow will spoil any sport I should think. Well, good luck to the fox! Major Brady is the Master, know him quite well. Lives about ten miles away.'

Over a very prolonged dinner with all the Christ-

186

mas trimmings, the conversation seldom waned, everyone being in good spirits. Then Diney brought up the subject of the mysterious train and its travellers, and told the vicar all about our experiences the previous night.

He and his wife were very impressed.

'I try to assure myself that my views are quite modern, but you know there are strange happenings that we cannot properly explain however much we like to try. For instance although many people may scoff about ghosts and apparitions there is often no other explanation for peculiar occurrences. Ghosts appear to be the wanderings of lost souls. Perhaps those who have died in odd circumstances. That is purely guessing, of course, but what other explanation is there?'

'You mean,' Julia said, 'those people we saw must have been ghosts? But we really did see them, and they left evidence of their presence, and why should we see them, why us?'

The vicar thought for a moment. 'I suppose it was a question of being in that place at the right time. Something triggered the event. You see, there must have been an occasion in the past, probably many years ago, when this event actually did happen, and what you saw was some kind of reincarnation of it.'

'You mean,' Julia persevered, 'that something happened years ago, perhaps something awful, something horrific, which brings these people, or I suppose I should say their ghosts, back to re-enact the actual deed or whatever it was.'

'Something like that, I suppose. Perhaps that train might have crashed and they were all killed. Who knows? It is all history now, but very intriguing. I suspect you won't be satisfied until you find out all

187

about it.'

'You did describe their dress, didn't you Julia?' Diney was really getting involved.

And Guy, not to be outdone, put in, 'And you described a funny little train, that should put some sort of date to it.'

'There you are, you see,' I said, 'we really are getting somewhere.'

Julia considered for a moment. 'Those clothes the people wore. Long dresses that we thought were fancy dress. They belonged to an era of some hundred years ago, that would be mid-Victorian.'

'Yes,' I interrupted, 'some of the men were in dress uniform, and if I am not much mistaken they were the kind the cavalry used to wear.'

'Right,' Guy said. 'Say about one hundred years ago, somewhere between 1850 and 1870. What was happening then?'

It was the vicar's turn.

'Well, 1853-1856 was the time of the Crimean war. The Charge of the Light Brigade and all that, when those gallant cavalry regiments were so much in the limelight. How about that?'

'That might well be, vicar, but what happened here at that time, at Brush of all places? I mean this is a very isolated spot really, and if what you say is right, there must have been some dreadful event right here to cause the reappearance of these long dead people. Perhaps only the old colonel will know the answer.'

The conversation dragged on for a while and then slowly dried up, as we could think of nothing else that might be pertinent.

The remainder of the evening passed most pleasantly in the manner that Christmas Day should be spent and the conversation became quite general

188

tending towards the verbose as we indulged in good food and wine. Diney and Guy were good hosts, and long standing friends to us, and so we had plenty of pleasant things to reminisce about. The vicar and his wife were good company too, and plainly interested in the many topics that we discussed.

We broke with tradition, later, inasmuch as the ladies stayed with the men as the port was passed around, and time passed swiftly, and it was soon afterwards that the clergyman reluctantly decided that it was time to say good-night.

'It has been along day, but a Christmas that I shall remember. You have also given us something to think about, it is a most interesting occurrence which I hope we shall resolve in due course. I am going to delve into the history of the village; who knows there might well be something that had become forgotten over the years. But you know what they say – "There are more things in Heaven and Earth" etcetera – and it is certainly true that the Good Lord moves in a most mysterious way. I have no doubt there is some good reason behind it all.'

After a night-cap we all retired to bed and slept well, and waking found that there had been a partial thaw during the night, the morning being dull and misty.

'We may see some hunting after all', Guy opined. 'The Meet is at eleven-thirty, and so I suggest we get along to the pub in good time.'

There was already a good crowd outside the Fox and Hounds when we got there, many with beer mugs and glasses in hand, for opening hours were relaxed on Boxing Day and Nobby was not averse to taking the locals' money on this occasion. There was a mixture of locals from the village and many of the gentry from the neighbouring area, and the lane was crowded with their cars.

We could hear the baying of the hounds which had not yet been released from their box so that the hunt servants could join with the crowd and enjoy their tipple. Already some of the horses were unloaded and were being saddled up.

As we strolled towards the assembly, Guy pointed. 'There's Major Brady – the Master, and look who he's talking to, that's old Colonel Fortescue, the chap we want to see.'

We pushed our way to where Guy had indicated, and as we approached the Master saw us and waved.

'Good morning, Guy, and how is the lovely Diney? Good to see you both and your friends.' He doffed his hard hat to the ladies.

'Good to be here again, Tim, let me introduce our guests and very old friends, Wing Commander Ian Johnson and his wife Julia. They are staying with us over Christmas.'

Diney turned towards the older man. 'And you are Colonel Fortescue, it has been most remiss of us not to have introduced ourselves before, although, of course, we have seen you at church and knew who you were.'

'The fault is equally mine,' the old soldier shook hands. 'Afraid I don't get about very much these days, not one for socializing, although I try not to miss the Meet, you know.' He smiled at Diney, and his rather austere and somewhat craggy face was suddenly transformed, and his eyes twinkled as he went on. 'It's not too often that I meet two such charming ladies in as many minutes.'

'You live at the top of the park over by the Hall,' I remarked in the pause that followed the colonel's gallantry. 'I was walking there yesterday afternoon trying to work off Mrs Harrison's splendid luncheon, and had a look at the ruins of the old Hall. I cannot resist poking my nose into old ruins, fascinates me trying to conjure what it once looked like, and all its history.'

I stopped speaking as I saw the old man's features seeming to close up. It appeared that this subject was taboo, and that he had no wish to continue with it.

But the situation was relieved when Major Brady, who either knew more about the situation, or sensed the old man's reluctance to discuss the subject of the Hall, spotted Nobby the landlord.

Calling him over, he ordered drinks. 'Pints for the men, all right? And how about the ladies? Something to keep out the cold, gin and tonic I think, Nobby.'

While we waited for the drinks we discussed the prospects of the imminent hunting. 'Not much scent, I suspect,' Tim Brady said. 'But never mind, a bit of exercise and fresh air will do everyone a bit of good after yesterday's over-indulgence.' He looked up as he heard his name called. 'Righto, Baines, be right over.'

Doffing his hat again to the ladies, he shook hands with us and the colonel. 'Must get along, seems it is time to move off.'

Colonel Fortescue was also about to leave us, but before he could excuse himself, Diney, using those wonderful eyes as only she knew how, managed to distract him from his intention.

'We were wondering if you would care to have a drink with us this evening and perhaps a very informal supper. As I said, it has been very remiss of us not to have invited you before, but we would very much like to remedy that. Boxing Day seems a very good time. Besides which I know that Julia and Ian would enjoy your company; make a change from talking to us.'

The old man was rather taken aback. Julia backed Diney up. 'Oh yes, do come Colonel Fortescue, we really cannot take "no" for an answer, can we Diney?'

'Putting it like that, how could I possibly do other than accept your very kind invitation. Indeed, it would be very nice.'

'Lovely, how about seven o'clock? As I said, quite informal, so don't dress up.'

Guy offered to collect him should he be unwilling to drive, but the old man dismissed the suggestion, inferring that he might be getting on a bit but was still quite capable of driving after dark.

The hunt moved off, quite a motley collection of adults and children, some in smart hunting clothes, some in rat-catcher, such was the informality of the Boxing Day Meet. Some decided to follow for a while, in cars and on foot, others decided to continue enjoying Nobby Crick's hospitality. We had another drink or two and then wended our way back to the Grange.

'The trouble with meals after Christmas is that they always seem to consist of cold left-overs, which really is a bit boring,' said Diney.

'So what, darling, do you suggest? Must do our guests proud, you know, said Guy, winking at Julia.

'Well, tell me,' our hostess ignored her husband, 'what does everyone really enjoy? Good home-cooking, nothing rich or complicated, tasty, and won't hurt your digestive powers! It so happens that I have, with my own fair hands, created –' We waited anticipating, no one daring to interrupt, playing Diney's game. She went on, 'A real culinary feat of country fare, suitable for all tastes – the original "cottage pie".' We all clapped enthusiatically, but she hadn't yet finished. 'Seasoned with herbs and garnished with mushrooms and shallots, accompanied by cauliflower "au gratin"; how's that?'

'Sounds marvellous,' I enthused, 'just right for Boxing Day supper, my mouth is drooling already!'

'Do you think that the colonel will like it?' Diney worried, 'he does not seem the gourmet type, but you never know.'

'Of course he will, all country people adore cottage pie,' said Guy. 'Good simple fare. Good excuse anyway to bring out the malt whisky, now that really is something, I will bet you that the old man will prefer that to wine!'

And so it proved. The old man's eyes lit up when he saw the bottle of Glenlivet.

'Just as it comes, please, don't want to spoil the taste,' he said as Guy proffered the ice.

'Quite right, sir; how about you, Ian?'

The dinner was a great success, and the colonel obviously appreciated the informality.

'Have you any family?' Julia asked him.

Just for a moment the colonel's eyes closed, and then he replied.

'No, not now. My only son, Tim, was killed in September 1940. His Hurricane crashed.'

Something clicked in my mind as the penny dropped. 'Fortescue,' I said, 'Tim Fortescue. I knew that the name was familiar. Of course.'

'You knew my son?'

'Yes sir, we were in the same wing at North Weald. We all knew him. He was a very brave man, you must have been very proud of him, we all were.'

The others were watching us, wanting to know

193

more. 'Have I your permission to tell them, colonel?'

With his somewhat reluctant consent, I told them how his son had refused to jump from his blazing fighter in order to steer it away from a town upon which it would have crashed, causing untold casualties, and perishing in the subsequent crash. 'He was given a posthumous V.C., one of the very few amongst the Few.'

I fell silent as an unshed tear glistened in the old man's eye.

'What a wonderful thing to do.' Diney, too, had tears in her eyes.

'Yes, of course. But then there were so many acts of self-sacrifice that autumn. So many brave young men went to their death unquestioningly.' He turned to me. 'But then you were there, too. You must have been one of those Few. We were proud of you all!'

He was lost in his own thoughts for a moment, no doubt that the Glenlivet had mellowed his memories, and he could probably think of his son as he had once known him. But his remarks about the Battle of Britain had conjured up my own memories, and made me somewhat embarrassed.

Diney no doubt sensed this, and chose the opportunity to change the subject. Addressing the colonel, she asked, 'Have you always lived in Brush? Nobby Crick, at the pub, inferred that you would know more about the village than anyone else.'

The colonel did not answer immediately, so Diney continued. 'We were wondering whether you could tell us of something that once happened here, many years ago, long before you were born. You see, Julia and Ian had a very strange experience on their way here on Christmas Eve.'

She went on to tell him how we had become lost in

194

the snow, and had ended up at the strange little station. Of the train and the fancy-dressed travellers. How we had returned there yesterday, and could still see the carriage wheel tracks and the horses' dung.

'You see, sir,' Guy chipped in, 'we were telling the vicar about it last night, and he was quite sure that it was some sort of manifestation, some re-enactment of something terrible that had happened in the past.'

We had the colonel's full attention now and he was staring at Julia and I.

'So, you have seen it too! Exactly what you have described appeared to me, once, long ago. It, too, was Christmas Eve. But as far as I have been able to ascertain no one else has ever witnessed it.'

He fell silent and then said, 'I think I owe you some sort of explanation, and a possible reason for what you saw. Oh yes, you saw ghosts – or whatever you care to call them – repeating a journey that they made almost exactly one hundred years ago. You were in the right place at precisely the right time, but further than that I cannot explain the whys and wherefores.'

He went on to tell us something about what had happened those many years ago.

'My grandfather, Julian Farley, was something of a railway pioneer, and he was building this railway, the remnants of which you saw. Then, he met and fell in love with a lady, the widow of a veteran of Waterloo. The Lady Emmerdale, who had been something of a recluse. He married her and set about rejuvenating Brush Hall. You see he was a very rich man. This was the time of the Crimea, you understand, and his new wife's younger son was a Balaclava hero.

'Well anyway this son returned home covered in glory and brought with him one of the nurses from the Scutari hospital. Apparently my grandfather,

195

Julian Farley, had a passionate affair with this girl, must have been something of a brainstorm as he was very much in love with his wife. Anyway, the upshot was that she had a child who was my father!'

We sensed that there was more to come, some tragic ending to this saga of years ago, and remained silent, unwilling to interrupt the telling.

After a pause he continued the story.

'Lady Emmerdale soon found out and sent the girl packing. Then, that Christmas, 1856, Julian Farley decided to have a grand ball, and the guests, or the ghosts of the guests that you saw, were arriving from London.

'But the very next day the younger son's ex-orderly turned up almost directly from the ship that had brought him back from the Crimea. And with him, unwittingly, he carried the dreadful cholera virus. He was what today we term a "carrier", he had had a slight attack and had recovered, but was still contagious.'

The colonel was apparently lost in his thoughts about the saga of another era, but after a minute or so continued.

'I really do not know why I should be telling you all this, about the tragedy that struck my grandfather's home; you are, after all until today, complete strangers, and I have never told this story to another soul. But you saw the ghosts and have some right to know the apparent reason for their appearance.'

'If this is painful to you in the telling,' Guy ventured, 'we will quite understand should you not wish to continue, but we are all quite enthralled, and, I have to admit, very curious as to what did happen in the end.'

'Oh, I am all right. You see my father, who was

196

killed on the Somme, passed the whole story on to me, and likewise I told my son, Tim. You see, he had the right to know, as, theoretically, my father was illegitimate, and even today this is looked upon as something not to be bandied about and to be kept in the family, so to speak. But, now, there is no more family, and when I go the whole wretched story will never be told again.

'Be that as it may,' he went on, 'the upshot was that the cholera was an extremely virulent disease in those days of poor hygiene, but little known in rural areas thus resulting in a lack of any immunity, but it was rife in the warmer climes of Europe and was widespread in the Crimea.

'Unfortunately no one of the family appreciated the danger that this soldier represented, until it was too late. How it was that he was allowed off the troopship when there were cholera victims aboard we shall never know. He was allowed to help in the kitchen which must have been foolhardy in the extreme. A day or so later the cook and a maid were taken ill, and died horribly within twenty-four hours. The younger son, the Balaclave hero, collapsed and his fiancée fled back to London.

'Apparently when the elder son, Gerald, the viscount, realized that his younger brother, whom he adored, was dead, in a fit of violent madness he disappeared across the park with my grandfather's shotgun.

'This was when Lady Emmerdale broke her neck falling down the stairs in a vain attempt to stop her son when she realized that he was about to kill himself.'

The silence in the room was pregnant in its intensity as the old man paused to gather his thoughts. Each of us found little difficulty in visualizing that dreadful scene of years ago. The horribly dead servants, the gallant cavalry officer, the old lady tripping on the stairs, and then from across the park, perhaps, the sound of the shotgun being fired.

'Then into this stricken house the young nurse, Fiona Fortescue – my grandmother – came, having been despatched post haste when the disease was first suspected. But she was too late. And then, search as they might they could find no trace of Sarah, the house maid. She had disappeared, in all probability had fled the stricken family.

'You can imagine the ghastly state of mind my grandfather, Julian Farley, was in. His adored wife was dead, he was beside himself with grief, and had no wish to continue his life without her. His ex-mistress, Fiona, was quite forgotten in his distress. All this grief had happened because of this horrible disease, and in this state of mind there was only one solution – a cure by burning. He set about setting fire to the house!

'It seems that he was half mad from grief and wanted nothing else but to die alongside his beloved Alice. He would have succeeded, too, only that he was dragged away by the old gardener and the groom.'

'Yes, old Ben told us that it was his great grandfather who helped pull him out, but did not know the reasons behind it all,' Guy said. 'But what about the viscount, Gerald? Did he really shoot himself?'

'Now, there's another story.' The colonel paused, and I took the opportunity to recharge the glasses. The Glenlivet had by now mellowed the old man, who now seemed to be enjoying his role of story-teller.

'The authorities were on the scene the next day, and although they searched the park, no sign of the viscount was ever found. And then there was the mysterious disappearance of Sarah, the house-maid. Apparently, by all accounts she was much taken by Gerald, and took every opportunity to fuss over him, after he had returned to the Hall from the mental institution where he had been recovering from the results of an hunting accident. She must have behaved very circumspectedly as it went almost unnoticed, although there had been rumours in the village that no one knew about until after this tragedy.

'So, I suppose that two and two were put together and might very well have made four. But neither she or the viscount were ever seen or heard of again. No trace of them has ever been found to this day!'